THEY CAME from BELOW

A Tom Doherty Associates Book
NEW YORK

THEY CAME from BELOW

Blake Nelson

THEY CAME FROM BELOW

A Tor Book
Published by Tom Doherty Associates, LLC
175 Fifth Avenue
New York, NY 10010

www.tor.com

Library of Congress Cataloging-in-Publication Data

Nelson, Blake.
They came from below / Blake Nelson.—1st ed.
p. cm.
Summary: While vacationing on Cape Cod, best friends Emily, age sixteen, and Reese, seventeen, meet Steve and Dave, who seem too good to be true, and whose presence turns out to be related to a dire threat of global pollution.
"A Tom Doherty Associates book."
ISBN-13: 978-0-7653-1423-9
ISBN-10: 0-7653-1423-1
1. Beaches—Fiction. 2. Marine pollution—Fiction. 3. Radioactive pollution—Fiction. 4. Pollution—Fiction. 5. Environmental protection—Fiction. 6. Imaginary creatures—Fiction. 7. Ocean bottom—Fiction. 8. Cape Cod (Mass.)—Fiction. I. Title.
PZ7.N4328The2007
[Fic]—dc22

2007009542

First Edition: July 2007

Printed in the United States of America

0 9 8 7 6 5 4 3 2 1

For Daniel Pinchbeck

We all walk in mysteries. We are surrounded by an atmosphere about which we still know nothing at all. We do not know what stirs in it or how it is connected to our intelligence.

—Goethe

Part ONE

(Associated Press) NOVA SCOTIA. — U.S. Navy officials confirmed today the loss of one of their prototype Baldwin "Hellfire" missiles somewhere in the North Atlantic.

The fully armed nuclear missile/torpedo hybrid was mistakenly fired from the submarine USS *Carlisle* during a training mission off the coast of Nova Scotia. It was lost at sea and has not been recovered.

Initial Navy reports indicated the missile did not detonate but that it may be leaking radioactivity.

Because of its high cost and extraordinary destructive power, the Hellfire missile remains one of the Navy's most controversial weapons systems.

The U.S. Coast Guard and other armed services were to assist with recovery efforts. By Saturday, however, the radioactive levels of the surface water were deemed too high to risk human exposure and the area was evacuated.

"We're actually very lucky the missile was lost in such a deep part of the ocean," observed one Navy spokesman. "The environmental impact will be limited to those lower regions. Hopefully fish and other wildlife that live near the surface will not be affected."

Environmental groups have called the loss of a damaged nuclear weapon the worst environmental disaster ever in the North Atlantic. Navy officials have refused comment.

One scientist on-site at the Halifax Marine Institute was quoted as saying: “Tuna and whitefish from the area have shown only a slight rise in toxicity levels. But I wouldn’t want to be down there where that missile is. That will be a formidable hot zone.”

1

"Cape Cod! Oh my god!" I said quietly to myself, staring out the airplane window. Of course it wasn't Cape Cod at all, it was just Boston harbor, but I was so excited to get there I couldn't help myself. I couldn't wait. I had been trying to concentrate on my summer-reading book, trying to do a crossword, but now I gave up on everything and just mashed my face against the little plastic window.

Soon Boston's downtown appeared beneath the airplane. It was much bigger than Indianapolis. It was much more complicated and tangled and just . . . *older,* I guess. I could see a stadium. Was it Fenway Park? Probably. There was a river that was brown and polluted looking. The whole city was brown and grimy and smoggy in the June heat. They were having a heat wave; I had been following it on the Weather Channel. As we got closer you could see the highways leading in and out of it, like arteries going to a heart.

We landed with a thump. I got off the plane and went downstairs and there was my dad at the baggage claim, looking tan and summery. I love my dad. It was so great to see him. He gave me a big hug and we carried my stuff to the car. Then, going out of town, we stopped at a Dunkin' Donuts and got delicious iced lattes and crunchy plain donuts.

I was so psyched to be going back to the Cape. My dad asked me about school and Indy and my mom, and we talked about everything. It was so fun to be riding along, letting my head lean back and watching the sun and the highway move past.

Then, after a couple hours, we got to the ocean. It was late afternoon and you could see the water through the trees and the sky was blue and the beach was so white and clean. We stopped at an overlook so I could do my ritual, which is: I get out of the car, take off my regular shoes, throw them in the backseat, and put on my flip-flops . . . *and the summer begins!*

The first thing I did in South Point—after I unpacked and had a cheese sandwich with my dad—was run down the street to see Reese Ridgley. Her parents were sitting on their front porch in their beach clothes, having their five o'clock cocktails. I said hi to them and asked them about their summer, but before they could answer I ran inside and up the stairs to Reese's room. She was there, folding her laundry. The minute she saw me she dropped her clothes and ran to me and we both jumped up and down and hugged and then stood back and looked at each other.

"Reese, oh my god!" I squealed.

"Emily Dalton! You're finally here!" she squealed back.

I, of course, lived in Indiana and she lived in Boston, so during the year we never saw each other. But now we were back in South Point for two whole months of fun in the sun—or whatever it was we did. Reese was not a typical beach-babe type. She was kind of Goth and dressed in black a lot. But I liked that about her. She was seventeen, a year older than me, and an East Coast girl, a city girl. When I told my friends in Indiana about her they thought she sounded like a freak. But I thought she was great!

After we calmed down, our first order of business was to walk into town and see who was around in terms of people our age and boys and the general tone of stuff. Our first stop was the Rad Shack. It was supposed to be a "serious" surf shop, but it made most of its money selling joke T-shirts and trendy flip-flops. We went in and looked around and I bought some sunscreen and a hat with orange flowers on it and Reese bought some sunglasses, which looked very punk, since she was already wearing black cutoffs and a DangerFactory T-shirt.

After that, we went across the street to Antonio's Meatball and Pizza Palace and ordered two "specials"—a slice and a Coke for $2.99. We flopped at a booth and breathed in the ocean air and the summer heat and watched a tourist family order different combinations of slices and Cokes (they could have just ordered three specials, but they didn't know how and spent twice as much money on the same thing).

Then Harold and Carl came in. They were local boys who worked at a garage at the edge of town. They had harassed us last summer, making fun of Reese mostly, calling her Miss Scary or Hairy Scary because she wore black and had really black hair on her arms. But they didn't say anything today. Maybe they had grown up and matured a little. Or maybe they just forgot who we were. They flopped at the booth closest to the door and watched the people on the sidewalk.

After Antonio's, Reese and I walked home along the beach. It was so beautiful and relaxing, with the sun on the water and a soft breeze blowing and our toes curling in the sand. Also, there seemed to be some cute guys around. Reese was especially psyched about that. She was determined to get some "boy action," as she called it. The summer before, we had blown it in various ways, mostly by being too shy or chickening out. But this year we were older and more mature and more determined. Boys, adventures, falling in love—whatever was going to happen, we were ready!

2

That night I made a special dinner for my dad, which was pork chops and rice and pineapple, which is his favorite—especially if you burn the rice a little.

My dad is so cool. He is a professor of marine biology at MIT in Cambridge, though he is now semi-retired and doesn't actually teach classes. He is older than most dads (he had me when he was forty-six), so he has white hair and he kind of limps around. He spends most days smoking his pipe and sitting on the porch thinking about science and the ocean. He has tons of books about philosophy and poetry and he listens to old jazz records that he keeps in a special cabinet where the sea air won't warp them. He lives about half the year in South Point. Everyone knows him and likes him. Once when his car got stuck in the sand, Sheriff Moshofsky and his deputy personally helped him get his car out, and they didn't charge him and after that they always called him "the Professor."

I should also tell about my mom. She's not as nice as my dad, but that's natural because she's my full-time parent, so she has to discipline me more and have a more practical approach to my future. I live with her, my two stepbrothers, and our dog in Indianapolis, which is nice if you like flat places that have no beaches. My mom and dad get along okay. She is much younger and had a second husband for a while (result: my younger stepbrothers), but then she got divorced from him, too, so there's a thing with my mom that she is pretty independent and also way smarter than your typical mom. That's how my dad met her; she was a brilliant student at MIT, though now she sells real estate around Indianapolis—not that that doesn't take brains, too; it's just different.

Anyway, so I made pork chops, rice, and pineapple for my dad and kind of messed up the pork chops because I hadn't cooked in a while. But I put a lot of extra pineapple on the pork chops and extra pineapple juice on our plates because that's the best part anyway. The wind had come up and there was a summer storm coming, so we turned down the lights and ate in candlelight while Dad listened to the BBC radio news. He likes the British news, I guess because British people are smarter and it's not just "murders and the weather" like American news.

When we finished dinner I cleaned up and Reese called and said we should walk on the beach because it was windy and spooky and there might be lightning later.

"You girls be careful," said my dad when Reese arrived. He went to the kitchen to make tea, but I insisted he sit down and I made it for him. I was still so happy to see my dad, it was the least I could do. Reese helped and then we all had tea, which is very civilized and British and good for you. Then Reese and I put on rain ponchos and walked to the beach to check out the storm.

3

During the next week Reese and I established our pattern for the summer: Wake up. Go to each other's house. Eat breakfast. Get our beach stuff. Go to the beach. Sit around and read magazines or whatever. Walk up and down the beach and check out boys. Go back home and take showers and put on moisturizer. Walk to Antonio's Meatball and Pizza Palace in the afternoon. Check in at the Rad Shack and say hi to the cute guy who works there (who was unfortunately twenty-five—too old—though Reese flirted with him anyway).

The only bad thing was if Harold and Carl spotted us. They were back to their old ways of harassing us. They would always say something crude or stupid, mostly to Reese, about her arm hair or her breasts (she had pretty big ones), which just proved how immature they were and how they secretly had a crush on her.

That was our day schedule. At night we would usually go to Reese's, because her parents had satellite TV and a DVD player. Some nights we hung out with my dad, because Reese thought he was the cutest dad ever and liked how distinguished he was and how he smoked a pipe. At my house we had to entertain ourselves without satellite TV, so we would lie on the floor and play cards or do tarot while my dad listened to old Charlie Parker records.

So one night, after about a week, Reese and I were at my house, playing gin rummy on the floor. At about ten-thirty, the phone rang. My dad answered it. We didn't usually get phone calls that late, so I noticed it and Reese and I both stopped playing our game.

"Oh, hello, Sheriff," said my dad.

Reese and I looked at each other.

My dad listened. He nodded his head. "I see," he said. "Well, sure, I could take a look. . . . All right. . . . About twenty minutes . . . ?"

He hung up the phone.

Reese and I both stared at him. "What did the sheriff want?" I said.

"Nothing. Just a dead seal or something washed up on Hadley Beach. They don't know what it is. They want me to come down."

Reese and I looked at each other. "Can we come?" I said.

"I don't know why you'd want to," said my father, getting his coat. "It's just going to be a dead animal carcass."

"We like dead animal carcasses," said Reese.

"It might smell bad," said my dad.

"We don't care," Reese and I said together.

"Well, if you feel like going for a ride."

Reese and I always felt like going for a ride. That was one thing about South Point in the summer. It was great and fun and everything, but very little actually happened. You had to grab any chance for excitement that came along.

We found some sweatshirts and got in my dad's Volvo. I sat in the front and Reese sat in back. We drove through South Point, where stupid Harold was sitting in his pickup truck, drinking beer and talking to some younger boys on bikes. Probably teaching them the finer points of harassing tourist girls.

We got to the highway and drove the eight miles to Hadley Beach. It was dark and the moon was big and glowing and gave everything that special moonlight shine. As we got closer you could see glimpses of the Atlantic through the trees. We came around a bend and suddenly you could see the whole ocean, silver and shimmering, the moonlight on the waves, far out to sea. Cape Cod was the most romantic place ever.

We pulled into the parking lot at Hadley Beach. I was surprised there were so many cars. There was a big white truck with the words HAZARDOUS MATERIALS on the side. There were two local cop cars and a Massachusetts State Police car. There was also a white van that had some official government logo on the door. It seemed like a lot of people for one dead seal. Reese, who was leaning forward between the two front seats, gripped my arm with excitement.

My dad parked and we walked to the wood staircase that went down to the beach. People were bunched at the top of the stairs, police and people on cell phones and walkie-talkies. They acted kind of paranoid. They wouldn't let us down, but my dad told them he was Professor Dalton and had been called by the sheriff. Even this didn't get him permission. Someone had to call someone on a walkie-talkie first. Down below, a crowd gathered around a thing that looked like a shiny white garbage bag. Farther along the beach there were other official people with flashlights looking at the beach and into the surf and not letting people walk through. Someone had a dog, and a policeman made him turn around and walk the other way. The dog was barking and freaking out.

Reese and I watched all this from the parking lot while my dad waited for permission to go down. Someone finally said okay and we started down the stairs, but the police stopped Reese and me. We were not allowed. We protested and complained to my dad, but he told us to wait in the car. We didn't want to, but more police had arrived and they began pushing everyone away from the edge of the parking lot. It was very strange. The cops were as curious as everyone else, so even as they told us there was nothing to see, they snuck looks at the white glob down on the beach.

Reese and I pretended to return to our car; then we ran to the other side of the parking lot and crept to the edge of the cliff overlooking the beach. From there we could see my dad. The policemen led him forward. People talked to him and talked into their walkie-talkies and someone with a very strong flashlight shone it on the white thing and it kind of sparkled and glowed in a strange way. Everyone stepped back with surprise. But not my dad. He bent down and touched it.

Then a helicopter came. I couldn't believe it. A real Coast Guard helicopter came down the beach and hovered above the parking lot. Reese and I were like *whoooa!* By now more police cars had arrived and some other official cars, Parks Department, et cetera. They made everyone drive their cars to one side, and landed the helicopter in the parking lot. It was superloud and dust and sand flew everywhere. Reese and I stayed hidden in the bushes by the edge of the cliff. We watched two paramedic guys jump out of the helicopter with a stretcher and hurry down the wood stairs. When they reached the bottom there was a big conference.

There were about thirty people now, gathered around the white thing. You could tell they weren't sure what to do. Finally the paramedics wrapped the white thing in an orange plastic tarp and rolled it onto their stretcher. They carried it up the stairs. Everyone wanted to help. The cops all followed the paramedics while they ran with it across the parking lot. They loaded the stretcher into the helicopter, and everyone stepped back. In another blast of sand and gravel, the helicopter lifted off the ground again. People had to turn away. When the helicopter was gone, everyone kind of stood around. One guy shone his flashlight on his hand and something must have happened, because everyone started looking at their hands. One guy started rubbing his hand on his pants.

We crept back from the cliff and returned to the car. My dad was waiting for us. He had a dazed look on his face. We were like, "What was that?"

He shook his head. "I have no idea."

"Was it a seal?" I asked.

"No," said my dad. "It wasn't anything like a seal."

"Was it alive?" asked Reese.

My dad shook his head again. "I . . . I'm not sure."

"Where are they taking it?" I said, looking into the sky.

"To the Coast Guard base. In Crutchfield."

"Are they trying to save it?"

"I assume so," he said. He looked at his hand. At the front of it and the back. We all looked. But there was nothing to see. "I need to talk to some of my colleagues," murmured my dad. "Let's go."

5

For the next couple days I listened to the news and watched the TV to see if they said anything about the white blob. Usually if they save something with a Coast Guard helicopter they put it on the news as one of those heartwarming stories about how nice humans are to animals. But there was nothing about it. Also, my dad went totally into science mode from that moment on. Like we got home that night and my dad went straight onto his computer and was talking on his phone and when I woke up the next morning he was still there, in the exact same place, reading printouts and answering the phone really fast when it rang. I went over to Reese's for breakfast, and when we stopped back on the way to the beach my dad had fallen asleep on the couch with his reading glasses still on. I took them off and put them on his desk. Reese lifted his feet onto the couch and we put a blanket over him.

At the beach that day Harold and some of the local boys were trying to surf. There must have been a storm or something, because the waves were totally huge. The lifeguards told people to be careful and put up warning flags, but Harold and Carl were back-talking them and disobeying, as usual.

Later that day some boys we didn't know sat near us and asked to borrow some sunscreen. We started talking to them. Their names were Nick and Justin and they were cousins from Australia. They were in South Point for three weeks on vacation with their parents. Reese told them that Antonio's was the main hangout and we could meet them there later, at eight, if they wanted. They said they couldn't because there was a soccer match they had to watch on TV.

So that was disappointing. But at least we had met someone. Later we walked into town and got specials at Antonio's and then got ice-cream cones at the little stand outside the General Store. We were sitting on the bench when Harold and Carl came by in their pickup truck. They pulled over and asked us if we wanted to come to a party. I shook my head no. But Reese was bored and said, "Where is it?" Carl said, "In my pants!" and they laughed and drove off.

We walked back to my house. Reese and I talked about boys from our high schools and what if we didn't meet any guys at all this summer? Last summer the closest thing we got to boyfriends were the Cohen brothers, who were in South Point for August and who we made out with a couple times at beach parties. Reese did anyway; I only kissed Michael Cohen once. But the Cohen brothers were super fun guys. They would decide to have a party and they would get beer and start a fire and find people to come, and it would totally be the best party ever. But where were they now? Reese and I didn't even know if they were coming this year. We sure hoped they would. We needed some interesting boys to show up. Otherwise, it would be an awfully dull summer.

6

The next day my dad spent all morning in front of his computer. He had calmed down somewhat; I was able to get him to have breakfast with me. He went outside to get the paper, and when he came back he said his leg and hip felt better than they had in years. He wasn't limping at all.

After that I went to Reese's, where her dad wanted us to help him paint the railing on their porch. We did that for a couple hours, and when it got too hot we walked to the beach. There we found the Australian boys, Nick and Justin, who were playing volleyball with some girls we didn't know. They invited us to play and we did, but Reese wasn't good at volleyball and I think she was a jealous that these new girls were hanging out with "our Aussies."

* * *

That night, Reese and I went to my house and lay on the floor and did tarot readings. My dad was on the computer, but something happened, because he got up from his computer suddenly and he was very upset and he called someone on the phone and talked to them in very heated terms.

"Dad?" I said when he got off the phone. "Are you okay?"

He rubbed his forehead. "Yes, honey, I'm fine."

"What was that thing on the beach, Professor Dalton?" said Reese. "Did they ever find out?"

"We don't know."

"Was it alive?"

"We don't know that, either. And now, unfortunately, it looks like we'll never know. They've cut off our access."

"Who has?"

"The federal government."

"Why would they do that?" I said.

"Because they're as baffled as the rest of us. People get touchy about things they don't understand. . . ."

"It sure was a strange color," said Reese, shuffling her tarot cards.

"It was very unusual, in a lot of ways," said my father. "It must have come from the very deepest part of the ocean."

"How deep is the ocean?" said Reese. "Hundreds of miles?"

"No. On average, three or four miles. But in some

places much more. Those are the interesting places. Those are the places where no human has been."

"I thought they had submarines," I said. "Little ones, with cameras?"

"Yes, but even those have not been to the very bottom."

"Wow," said Reese. "So anything could be down there? And we wouldn't even know?"

"Precisely," said my dad. "Which is why this discovery is so important."

"How about fish?" I said. "Aren't there special fish who can go super deep?"

"That's why it's so interesting, and so important," said my dad. "We really have no idea who or what might be down there."

Reese put away the tarot cards and shuffled the deck of normal cards.

"But why would they deny access to it?" I asked. "Every new discovery helps science in some way, doesn't it?"

"New discoveries are just that," said my dad. "They're new. Whether they're good or bad for science, or for people in general, that's the thing you never know."

That was an odd thing for my dad to say. Usually he thought all knowledge was good. "You think it might be dangerous?" I said.

"I can't say. There's no way to tell. If they don't let us study it . . ."

Reese and I played normal cards for a while. My dad was still upset and the whole mood of the night was strained. Reese decided to go home. I offered to walk her home because it had gotten cold and foggy. It was awfully weird weather lately. But she said she wanted to go by herself. She felt like walking; she wanted to think about her tarot reading, which had said that a very significant birth would occur that would change the course of her life. Or something like that. I never understood tarot. It was more Reese's thing.

I lent her a coat and walked her to the road. We said good-bye and I went back inside, where my dad was talking to someone on the phone, demanding something and arguing. The thing is, my dad never yells or argues or does anything like that. It was scary to hear him so angry. It was a very strange night.

It got stranger. I went to bed and got out my copy of *Us Weekly* and turned on my little bed light. I was reading about how different celebrities like their Starbucks coffees, but then I heard something out my window. It was a clicking sound. Then a muffled voice. I turned off my light for a second and listened. There was another click, another muffled voice. I crept to the window and very carefully pulled the curtain aside. My heart was totally pounding, but then I saw it was only Reese, waving from the other side of the hedge.

I quietly opened the window. "What are you doing?" I whispered.

"Oh my god, you have to come!"

"What is it?"

"Just come; I have to show you something."

"What is it?" I said.

"On the beach."

"Tell me what it is!" I said. But I was already pulling on my jeans. I opened the window more and crawled out. I crept quietly around the hedge. I got to where she was and she grabbed me and led me around the front of the house. Inside, I could see my dad still working on his computer in the living room.

I generally didn't do anything bad at the beach, but I did love sneaking out of the house. We had done it a couple times last summer when we got bored. So even if Reese didn't really have anything to show me, it was still fun.

"Oh my god, wait until you see this," she said when we got to the road. She was walking very fast.

I hurried to keep up with her. "What is it?" I asked.

"People having sex!" she said.

7

"Reese!" I protested. "I don't want to see that!"

"I know, but just come," she said, dragging me along.

This had happened last summer. While walking home on the beach one night, we thought we saw two people having sex in the dunes above the beach. I didn't want to go near them. But Reese had wanted to get closer. I mean, Reese wasn't a pervert or anything. She didn't want to go *stare* at them; she just liked the idea of it. She wanted a glimpse. She was more curious about sexual things than I was.

"I'm not watching people have sex!" I repeated.

"They're probably just making out," said Reese. "You can't even see them anyway; they're in the bushes."

"You are such a sex fiend sometimes."

"Don't you want to have sex someday?"

"Yeah, but not in the bushes of South Point! And not with people *staring* at me."

But I went with her. We walked down the road and onto the beach. We walked along the water awhile, until we came to a flat grassy place above the dunes. In one spot there was a dense thicket of bushes and trees.

"How did you even see them?" I whispered as we approached.

"I saw the bushes moving."

"How did you know what they were doing?"

"I could see their naked feet. And part of their legs."

Maybe they're just wearing shorts," I said.

Reese stopped. She looked into the bushes. "Actually, I think it might have been two guys."

I stopped dead. "Two *guys*?"

"I know," said Reese. "But whatever, we're not going to look; we're just seeing if they're actually there."

"And why are we doing that?" I asked.

"To see if I really saw something or not."

"I don't care if you really saw something or not!" I said. "What if it's homeless people or weird hippies or something? What if they kidnap us?"

But there was no stopping her. She trudged through the sand and climbed up the dune about a hundred feet from the thicket. I crawled up behind her, just high enough to see over the dune. She pointed into the bushes. "That's where they were."

"You want to see? Go ahead," I said. "I'm staying right here."

"Oh, come on."

"No way, Reese!"

"All right. Just wait." She crawled onto the flat grassy area and crept silently to where the thick bushes created a little fortlike space. I had to admit, it was a perfect make-out spot. You could have a small party in there and no one could see.

Reese didn't go into the bushes; instead she circled around the outside trying to see inside.

I watched her. I checked behind me to see if anyone was by the water. It was after midnight and cold, so the beach was deserted.

When I turned back, Reese had gone around to the other side. I couldn't see her anymore. The night had gotten very still, except for the quiet wash of waves and that big empty sound the ocean has. I waited for Reese to reappear. I heard something stir in the grass to my left. I caught my breath. But it was only the wind.

I waited. This was so ridiculous. I did not want to spend my summer waiting around for Reese to get herself into trouble. I stared at the tangle of trees and bushes. That was a bad idea, though, because in the dark my eyes invented things. Like part of a tree stump suddenly looked like a thick black troll, crouched down, hiding, waiting to pounce and devour any dumb teenagers who happened to wander by.

Then something cold touched my bare ankle. I just about jumped out of my skin. But it was only sand slipping down the dune. I tried to calm myself down. Obviously there was no one in the bushes. Even if someone had been doing something, they wouldn't still be there now.

I thought about the Australian boys Nick and Justin. Since we were out, maybe we could walk down to hotel row; maybe they would be hanging out somewhere and we could find them. . . .

That's when I heard the scream.

8

Reese wasn't a good screamer. She didn't have a high, piercing voice. Her version of a scream was more like a shout with no air in it, followed by several little yelps that were confusing, like was she hurt or just freaking out or what?

Whatever it was, she came sprinting around the bushes right at me. At first I thought she might be joking or trying to scare me. But when she got closer and threw herself off the dune and went rolling past me to the beach, I knew she was truly frightened.

"Come on! Come on!" she yelled breathlessly.

"What was it?" I said, jumping down to her.

"Ohmigod!" She continued to run. "It was a body!"

"A *body*?" I was running now, too.

"Or something. It was a leg. It was naked. And blue."

"Was it just a leg? Was the rest of it there?"

She nodded yes. We kept running, but it was hard in the sand. When we got to the tourist parking lot, we ran up the ramp toward the restrooms. Reese grabbed the pay phone. She dialed 911. Reese was panting so much she had trouble telling the police where we were. But they figured it out. They said a squad car would be there in two minutes.

It was. Driving it was a guy named Luke, who I remembered from last summer. He was the nephew of the sheriff. Luke was only twenty-two and kind of a jerk sometimes. We were still very glad to see him, though. He had his deputy sheriff uniform on. He also had his friend there, Jimmy. I had seen Jimmy around Antonio's. He was dressed in normal clothes now, but he had a gun and a holster, which he put on while Luke told his radio dispatcher that he was "on-scene."

Reese led the way. We all trudged back through the soft sand to where the thicket was. While we walked I caught Jimmy checking Reese out. He was looking at her body. He even made a little gesture to Luke, who gave him a stern look, like this was serious business, not a time to be hitting on girls.

Reese pointed into the bushes where she had seen the leg. She and I waited while Luke and Jimmy crawled up the dune. Jimmy wasn't the best crawler. But they were into the whole police thing and having guns and all that; you could tell. Reese wanted to watch, so she followed them to the edge of the dune. I wasn't going to get left behind, so I did, too.

Once on the bluff, Luke and Jimmy approached the thicket with their flashlights on. Probably Luke had been there before, busting people for partying or illegal camping. He seemed pretty calm. He looked back to make sure it was the right place. Reese nodded her head that it was. Luke talked into his radio and started around one way; Jimmy went the other. Reese and I waited.

"Was it dead?" I whispered.

"Yes."

"But how do you know?"

"Because it was blue."

"Real blue?"

"No, like white but with a blue tint."

"Was it a boy or a girl?"

"It was a boy, I think," said Reese.

"You think?"

"I don't know. But it was totally a real leg, a human leg," she said, getting mad.

"Okay, okay," I said.

I heard Luke's radio blast static. He said, "I'm not seeing anything. We have the two witnesses here. . . ."

"I am *not* a witness," I told Reese. "If my dad finds out I'm down here . . ."

"Calm down," she said. She stood up and waved to Luke that he wasn't far enough to the left.

Then something happened. Luke turned suddenly as if he'd heard something move.

"Jimmy?" he called out.

"Luke!" came the answer. "I got something!"

"What! What is it!"

"It's a . . . it looks like . . . holy crap, it's *not dead!*"

A shot rang out. It was so loud and scary my heart almost stopped.

"Jimmy!" screamed Luke. "Jesus! Don't shoot!" He reached for his own gun. He dropped his flashlight as he struggled to get the gun out of the holster.

Something did move somewhere. You could hear it in the bushes. Luke was trying to move backward and draw his gun at the same time. He almost fell. Whatever was in the bushes didn't sound big, though; it sounded dog-sized or like a deer. I thought, *My god, they're going to shoot someone's dog and we'll all be in huge trouble.*

"Jimmy! Where are you!" shrieked Luke, who now sounded scared as well as angry.

Another shot rang out. It was so close and so loud, Reese and I both ducked down. When we lifted our heads Luke was running around to the other side. He looked terrified. His flashlight and hat were on the ground. His radio, which was attached to his shoulder, was dragging in the grass on its cord.

"Jimmy!" he screamed. He disappeared behind the thicket. "Where are—!"

There were two more shots and then a low thud, like something hitting the ground. It sounded terrible. It sounded like a person.

When I dared to lift my head again, Luke was running straight toward us, just like Reese had done. He was coming so fast all I could do was duck, and sure enough, he ran right over us and tumbled down the dune.

Reese ran to him. She tried to help him up. "Oh god oh god oh god . . . ," he mumbled. "I shot him. I shot Jimmy. I shot him in the chest . . . !"

He looked for his radio, but all he could find was the cord. He couldn't find the part you talk in. *"Oh god oh god oh god . . . ,"* he babbled.

"Luke, Luke!" said Reese, trying to calm him. "Try to think! What should we do?"

He didn't answer. He stumbled to his feet. He'd lost

his gun, his hat, his flashlight, everything. He turned and started running down the beach toward his car.

Reese and I stood there. Reese looked back to the thicket. I was like, "No way are we going up there."

"We have to. What if Jimmy's dying?" She climbed up the dune. I went, too. When we got to the top we crept toward the thicket. It was the scariest thing I had ever done. Suddenly Reese flinched.

"What?" I said.

"I saw something!"

"What?" I said, ducking down in the grass.

"Something over there." She pointed into the trees behind the thicket.

I saw it, too. It was like a ghost. It was white and luminous and it moved in a weird way.

"What is that?" said Reese.

"It must be a deer," I said. "They have white tails."

"That is *not* a deer," said Reese.

"What else could it be?" I said.

Reese stared forward, but whatever it was, it had disappeared.

"God, I am *sooo* going to be in trouble," I said. But we couldn't leave Jimmy alone in there. We crept forward.

Thankfully, just as we got to the thicket, an ambulance came driving up the beach, alongwith a police car. Reese and I immediately snuck off to the side where they wouldn't see us. Luke was in the police car, but he didn't come out. Some other guys ran up the dune toward the thicket with their guns out. The ambulance guys followed with a stretcher.

"I'm going home," I whispered to Reese. "Before my dad finds out."

"Okay," she whispered back. "I'm going to stay. I'll call you in the morning."

10

The next morning I had to act like everything was normal. I got up and made breakfast. My father continued to work at his desk and talk on the phone. I casually turned on the radio, but there was nothing on the news—at least nothing about Luke and Jimmy. I made tea. The Cape Cod paper came and I looked at it, but there was never anything in it except old Mrs. Gilroy was selling her dishwasher.

Finally, Reese showed up. I told my dad I was going to town and he didn't even look up from his computer. Outside on the street we both walked fast. Reese looked tired and stressed; I'm sure I didn't look much better. The minute we were away from my house I got the whole story. Reese had stayed and seen it all.

The news was good. The policemen had crawled into the thicket and at first couldn't find anything. But then Jimmy appeared. He was standing in the long grass a few yards away. Everyone was surprised but very relieved. Jimmy was in shock and they walked him to the ambulance. The paramedics checked him for gunshot wounds, but there were none. Luke must have missed. But the weird thing was: Jimmy had a wound in his chest. It wasn't a gunshot; it was like someone had stabbed him with a sharp stick. He was also totally in a daze. He didn't remember anything, getting shot at, or what had happened, or if he saw a body. Nothing.

After that, all the other deputies went into the thicket and they brought a police dog and went all through it. The dog barked a lot, but no one could figure out what had happened or if anything was in there. They finally asked Reese if she was absolutely sure she had seen a body in there. She told them she wasn't.

I gripped her arm. "But Reese, you *did* see something. And what about that white thing we both saw?"

"I couldn't tell them that," she said. "They would think I was making it up. And we almost got Jimmy killed. They didn't want to look for bodies anyway. They wanted to go home."

At Antonio's, we sat in a booth and ate two specials each. It was an overcast day, so people were in town. Harold and some of his crew drove by in their truck.

"So they just decided to forget about it?" I asked.

"I guess so; I don't know."

"That is so weird."

"How do you think *I* feel?" Reese said.

Harold came in with his buddy Carl and they got specials. "Hey, ladies," said Harold. "How's it hanging?"

We ignored them.

"Or maybe you should ask us that," said Harold, much to his own amusement.

"Could you guys be more retarded?" said Reese.

"Uh-oh! She's getting scary!" said Carl.

"Hairy Scary!" said Harold.

"Hey, Reese," said Carl. "Wanna go into the dunes with me tonight? I got something I want to show you. It's kinda scary. I think you'll like it."

"Sure you could find it in the dark?" said Reese.

Everyone laughed, including a couple Antonio employees.

"Whoa, dude," Harold said to Carl. "I think you just got facialized!"

Later Reese and I went across the street. Nick from Australia was at the Rad Shack buying some yellow-tinted sunglasses. That cheered us up. We talked to him and he said some people were having a beach party on Saturday night, if it wasn't too cold. We said we would go, definitely. After that we felt better about things and anyway, whatever happened in that thicket, it wasn't any of our business. We were just tourists. We were just on vacation.

11

Saturday night Reese and I went to the beach party. It was a little cold, so we wore jeans and sweatshirts, and Reese wore black eyeliner and her red-checked Vans that had writing around the edges of the soles. I just had my boring Nikes, but I was from the Midwest, so whatever.

We found the party. Nick and Justin had built a big fire. Nick introduced us to his sister, Sheila, who was very friendly. Also some of the girls who had played volleyball were there, which wasn't so great. I didn't care that much, but Reese was jealous. Not that we wanted to hook up with Nick and Justin, but they were the cutest boys in South Point so far. In any event, we were at a disadvantage since we actually lived in South Point for the summer and they were staying on hotel row. South Point people made fun of hotel row, but it was where the most partying was, because the people there were only around for a week or a weekend.

Nick and Justin didn't seem like super-party types, though. They weren't sleazy, and the girls were nice, too. We all sat around the fire and more people showed up with beer. Reese and I didn't know these people, either, but they were cool. It was kind of funny because Reese was so Goth and everyone else was more normal and preppie. But everyone got along and someone had a boom box and we listened to music. Eventually Justin talked to Reese about Marilyn Manson. He asked her what his deal was—assuming Reese was into him because of how she dressed. Reese wouldn't give Justin a straight answer, which meant she liked him. Maybe she was going to have a summer boyfriend after all.

Then Sheila, Nick's sister, said we should all go swimming. I looked at Reese. It was totally dark and the ocean was black and not exactly inviting. But Nick and Justin weren't afraid; they both stripped to their boxers and ran to the water. Sheila and a couple of the volleyball girls followed, also stripping to their underwear. Reese and I were left at the bonfire with the other less brave people.

"Should we go?" I whispered to Reese.

"You can go."

I wasn't going. I nestled my fists inside my sweatshirt. One of the other boys said, "Did you hear about that dude who was sneaking around last night?"

We hadn't. He told us some people in his motel had seen someone looking in their window in the middle of the night. They complained and a bunch of other people said the same thing. And also, the dogs had barked until after midnight. When they called the hotel manager he said it was nothing and the dogs were only barking because they were city dogs and didn't know the smells of the ocean. But the boy said his own dog was going crazy, like he had never seen the dog do—and he had been to the ocean lots of times.

"What did people think they saw?" asked Reese.

"They figured it was some pervert," said the boy, "looking in their window."

12

People talked more about the prowler. One of the other boys who wasn't swimming smiled at me, but by that point I was totally thinking about Nick. Not that he liked me back, but I'd already reached that point: Nick or no one. Which was kind of lame, I know. But that's how I am about guys. I can only like one at a time.

Meanwhile, people came running back from the ocean. They were freezing of course and ran to get near the fire. Justin and Nick were shivering and dripping on everyone. The girls who had swum were covered in goose bumps and grabbing their towels, since their soaked underwear was pretty much see-through at that point.

Later a bunch of the girls took off. So then it was more like eight or nine of us. Reese and Justin began talking and ended up sitting by themselves. It seemed like Reese might be into Justin. Which was good for her but would put pressure on me. In a way.

Sheila and the other people drank beer. People began to snuggle under blankets. I talked to Sheila for a while. Then Nick came and talked to us. He was very respectful and a little shy. I wondered if he could like me. It seemed possible.

Then Harold and Carl came walking along the beach. Of course, they couldn't just mind their own business; they had to join the party. The other people didn't know how obnoxious they were and someone gave them a beer. I knew they would eventually insult someone or belch or do something gross. But it wasn't too bad. They drank and complained a little. Carl tried to chat with one of the girls. She wouldn't really talk to him. So they complained some more and Harold spit in the fire and they left.

Sheila said, "Who are those guys?"

"They're locals," I said. "They're not very nice."

"Do you want one of these?" said Sheila, holding up a beer.

"No thanks," I said.

Nick did, though. He took it and lay beside me. He made a pillow with his coat so he could look toward the water.

"Do you ever think about the ocean?" he asked me.

"What about it?" I said.

"Like what could live down there? Like how there's as much life down there as up here? Maybe more?"

"God Lives Underwater," said someone. "That's the name of a band. They're awesome."

"But seriously," Nick said, "it's like an alternate universe. Right here on our own planet."

"Right here, a hundred feet from us," said Sheila.

"Right here in my hair," said one of the girls who had swum, pulling some sea gunk out of her wet hair.

Everyone laughed quietly at that. Nick drank his beer. The wood crackled as it burned. We all stared at the black ocean.

13

The next day was sunny and hot and everyone went to the beach. Reese and I found Nick and Justin and Sheila and put our towels with theirs. We were totally friends now. Later we swam with them and bodysurfed and had water fights.

I, of course, stayed near Nick and talked to him as much as possible, not just in a girl-boy way but also because he was smart and the most fun person to talk to. Reese, though, was totally ignoring Justin, which was making him mad. I suspected it was an act. Reese was tough on boys. She liked to make a guy work a little. Especially if he was cocky like Justin.

Later some of the volleyball girls showed up, with

some boys of their own (thank you). One of them mentioned that the cop in the parking lot was giving people a hard time and checking their coolers for beer. Reese asked him which cop it was and he said it was Luke.

So later, when we got bored, Reese and I walked up to the parking lot and found Luke sitting in his police car. He was not happy to see us. He was embarrassed, I guess, since we had seen him freak out.

"Hey, Luke," said Reese.

He squinted at us and put his sunglasses on.

"Sure is a nice day," said Reese.

"What do you want?" said Luke. He was writing something in his police notebook.

"Just wanted to say hi. See if you're okay."

Luke said nothing.

"That sure was weird the other night," said Reese.

"Weird nights are what I do. That's police work."

Reese didn't say anything. I watched him write. I felt a little sorry for him. He was too young to be really "authoritative" or policelike, though he sure tried.

"Did you hear about that guy looking in people's windows?" said Reese. "On hotel row?"

"Of course I heard about it. I'm the local cop."

"Well, what happened?"

"We checked it out. It was nothing."

"Lotta weird stuff going on around here," said Reese.

"Nothing we can't handle," said Luke.

"And Jimmy's okay?" said Reese.

"Jimmy's fine."

"You were so scared . . . you were so sure . . ."

Luke looked hard at her. She stopped talking.

"Sorry," she said.

"Those kids, those Australians, are they drinking alcohol on the beach at night?" asked Luke.

Reese played dumb. "Not that I know of."

"If they do and I catch them, I'll take them in. And their parents can pay the two-hundred-dollar fine. Will you tell them that for me?"

"Sure, Luke."

He gave Reese a hard look, like he thought she was insulting him somehow. But she wasn't.

The rest of the day, Reese and I mostly lay on our towels or swam. There were a lot of people on the beach. It was the second week of July, which was pretty much the best week in terms of good weather and big crowds.

"Poor Luke," said Reese as we walked back to our towels.

"Yeah," I said.

"That night, at the thicket, I was sure he'd shot Jimmy. I was positive."

"I know," I said. "I thought I heard the actual bullet, hitting something. Like a thud."

"Really?" said Reese. "You heard that, too? I just figured that's what guns sounded like."

"It must have been something else," I said. "Since he's fine."

"Except he did have that wound in his chest."

"Yeah, what was that?"

"I don't know," said Reese. "I didn't see it myself. He was in the ambulance. I just heard them talking about it."

"That night was so weird," I said.

"It was the weirdest."

"I'm just glad we're here, and hanging out with Nick and Justin. And everybody's okay."

"Yeah," said Reese. "Me, too."

14

That night it seemed like everyone was in town. Antonio's Meatball and Pizza Palace was packed; the Rad Shack was open and full of people; the General Store was so crowded you could barely get inside. Reese and I waited in line at the ice-cream stand and got double cones and found a bench in front of the post office. It was a relief to sit. We were pretty fried from being in the sun all day.

We ate our ice creams in silence, watching the people walk by. I was spacing out when Reese suddenly nudged me with her elbow. Two guys were coming up the street. They were coming in our direction. Reese nudged me again as they got closer.

"Check these guys out . . . ," she whispered. I already

was. They were the cutest guys I had ever seen in South Point. They were the cutest guys I had ever seen *anywhere*. They were like two young Brad Pitts. I swear to god. They looked just like him. It was too weird. I literally blinked my eyes and looked again.

Reese stopped eating her ice cream. I stopped eating mine. They wore jeans and old beach shirts and flip-flops. They were tan and both had movie-star haircuts, Brad Pitt haircuts. I actually expected to recognize them at any second. They had to be celebrities, or people made up to look like celebrities. Or maybe they were models; maybe they were doing a fashion shoot on the beach. Not that anyone did that in South Point. It wasn't that nice of a beach.

Reese elbowed me again. They were almost in front of us. Maybe they were from Europe. They kind of walked funny. And they had odd expressions on their faces. The shorter one was looking down and kind of frowning, like he was in pain or had hurt himself. The taller one looked around, but in a stiff, awkward way.

"Hey," Reese called out when they were in front of us.

I was so nervous I almost crushed my ice-cream cone in my hand. The tall guy stopped and the pained guy stopped, too. They had the strangest body movements; the tall guy had to turn his whole body to look at us.

"Hey, where are you guys from?" said Reese, laughing slightly to cover her nervousness. "Not from around here, I bet."

They both stared at us. They both looked like movie stars. They had to be brothers. They were *soo* not from around here.

"Hello," said the tall one.

"Hello to you, too," said Reese.

A car came down the street and they stepped closer to the sidewalk, closer to us.

"Are you guys models or something?" I heard myself say.

"Emily," whispered Reese.

"What?" I said.

"Don't say that."

"What?" I said back. "It's okay to ask someone that."

Reese turned to them. "Well, are you?" she asked.

"We are . . . not models," said the taller one.

"Are you brothers?" said Reese. "You must be brothers."

The taller one looked at us. The shorter one made a grimacing face. "We are not brothers."

"What country are you from?" said Reese a little more seriously.

"We are . . . from this . . . country," he said.

"Why do you talk so weird?"

"Are we talking weird?" said the tall one. His speech sort of changed, like he had suddenly figured out how to talk in a normal speed and cadence. His body seemed to change slightly as well. Like something in his face sort of . . . grew. Not much, but just enough that something was different. Suddenly he was a little less good-looking than he was a second before. And he was a little taller. And his friend was a little shorter. And suddenly they could talk like normal people. It was the strangest thing. Obviously, I had had too much sun that day. And too much sugar.

"You talk like foreigners," said Reese.

"Do we? It must be because . . . we have been studying in a foreign country."

"I guess," said Reese. "What's wrong with your friend?"

The shorter guy was bending over like he had a stomach cramp. He was gripping one of the wood posts that held up the awning of the post office.

"Is he okay?" asked Reese.

"Yes," said the taller one, who did nothing to help his friend. "It is something in his digestive tract. He has a pain there."

"Does he talk?"

"Yes. Of course."

"You guys are totally from Germany or someplace," said Reese. "You're not Americans. I can tell a German accent."

"Yes . . . ," said the tall one. "We have been studying in Germany. We have been in Germany a long time."

The other brother seemed to recover from whatever was wrong. He stood up straight and smiled strangely at us.

"What are your names?" said Reese.

They looked at us. The taller one answered. "My name is Steve. His name is Dave."

"Steve and Dave," repeated Reese suspiciously. "You're sure about that?"

I looked closely at the tall one. He really had changed. He really was not as good-looking as he had been a minute ago. But now he looked more . . . trustworthy or wholesome or likeable or something.

It was weird because that happens sometimes. Like if you meet someone who looks conceited, if you talk to them and they turn out to be really nice, they actually look different to you. They seem to soften. But this was different. This person had actually *changed.* He had changed his face. And it wasn't the sun or my own lack of sleep. This really happened, right there, as we were talking. I was sure of it.

15

Reese had the great idea to take Steve and Dave to Antonio's. I think she wanted to get them inside, where she could get a better look at them. I did, too. Also, they seemed so friendly and open. They had this pleasant way that made you want to hang out with them, even though they were about the oddest people we had ever encountered. Also, I think Reese wanted to show them off. She made a point of walking past the Rad Shack and waving to the cute guy who worked there.

Inside Antonio's, the first thing Reese and I wanted to figure out was how old Steve and Dave were. It was hard, though. You couldn't tell by their faces, which were sort of bland and unclear. They could have been seventeen, or they could have been twenty-seven. They had strange skin, too, very clear and an odd color, tan but more brown than actually tan from the sun. I found myself wishing I could touch them. But of course that would have been too weird.

Antonio's had cleared out a bit. It was mostly young people, hanging out and chewing on their pizza crusts. Carl was there with his friends. Harold wasn't, which was good. Reese and I got $2.99 specials. Steve and Dave both said they weren't hungry; they didn't want anything. Reese said they should get a slice. Steve said they didn't have any money. So Reese bought them a slice.

We sat with them in a booth. Carl and some of those guys came up to the counter to get more Cokes. They kind of stared at us. I thought they might do something or say something, but they didn't. They just stared. Reese ate her pizza, I did, too, since we were hungry from our long day at the beach. Steve and Dave mostly looked at their pizza slice. Steve picked it up at one point and smelled it and put it down.

"I know; it's not the best pizza," said Reese. I think she had decided she liked Steve, even though Dave was darker in his eyes. They didn't look nearly as identical as they had on the road. But there was something about them that was still very attractive. It was fun to sit with them. I realized I had a big smile on my face. I had been smiling constantly since we first saw them.

Dave groaned. He bent over like he was going to be sick. "Are you okay?" said Reese, reaching over and touching his shoulder.

"He is fine," said Steve, moving her hand away. Dave remained bent over for a moment, then sat up and seemed to recover. He said, "I have pain in my stomach sometimes."

"That's okay," said Reese. "I get that sometimes. Cramps. You know."

Steve wasn't paying attention. He was looking at his pizza. He touched the melted cheese. He looked at his finger.

"I know," said Reese. "It's too greasy. The pizza in Boston, where I'm from, is much better."

"So what are you guys doing here?" I said.

"We are . . . ," said Steve.

"We're looking for someone," said Dave.

"Who?" said Reese.

"No one," said Steve. "He just means a friend of his is staying nearby. And we hope to run into him."

"Oh," said Reese, grinning and chomping into her pizza. She didn't seem to care that everything Steve and Dave said was totally bizarre. They were *sooo* cute, and I guess that was the important thing.

16

As we left Antonio's, Reese was bumping up against Steve and touching him on the arm. She totally liked him. She asked him how old he was as we walked into the street. But before he could answer he tripped and fell. I don't know what he tripped on. He fell awkwardly, on his hands and knees, and when he stood up he stared at his hands, which were skinned and bleeding slightly. Reese, of course, helped him up and brushed him off. She couldn't keep her hands off him. It was a little embarrassing.

Then I heard someone call my name. I turned and saw Luke across the street, sitting in his police car. Jimmy was in the passenger seat. It was the first time Reese and I had seen Jimmy since the night at the thicket. We steered Steve and Dave toward the police car to say hi. Steve and Dave stood back while Reese and I leaned into the car.

"Hey, Jimmy," I said. It was awfully nice to see him sitting there, alive. He looked a little embarrassed, though.

Luke had his sunglasses on. Reese immediately teased him about it, and he took them off. I realized that Luke had a slight crush on Reese. Who didn't?

"So who are your friends there?" said Luke, nodding his head at our escorts.

"Oh, this is Dave and Steve," said Reese, stepping back and gesturing to them to come closer to the car. They moved slightly closer.

"Are they drunk?" said Luke.

"No, no, they're just klutzes," said Reese, leaning back into the police car and smiling broadly.

"What are you so happy about?" said Luke.

"Nothing," said Reese, smiling and bouncing slightly on the balls of her feet.

"Where are they from?" said Luke.

"They're from Germany. I mean, they're Americans, I guess, but they've been going to school in Germany."

"*Sprechen Sie Deutsch*?" Luke said to Steve.

Steve seemed surprised by this. "Uh . . ." he said. "*Ja, ich spreche Deutsch. Ich habe es einige Jahre lang in der Schule gelernt.*"

He waited for Luke to say something back, but of course Luke didn't know German. He only knew "*Sprechen Sie Deutsch.*"

"See? They speak German," said Reese. "They're very smart."

"They ought to learn how to walk," said Luke. "Where are they staying?"

"Where are you staying?" Reese asked them.

Everyone looked at Steve and Dave. Everyone except me. For some reason I looked at Jimmy. He had this incredulous look on his face, like he recognized Steve and Dave, like he knew who they were. His mouth actually fell open for a second.

Steve and Dave avoided the question of where they were staying. Or maybe they were so new in town they didn't remember where their hotel was. They pointed vaguely inland. But Luke had lost interest anyway. A call was coming over the police radio about a car in a beach parking lot playing its stereo too loud. Luke frowned and told the dispatcher he would check it out. He started the police car and revved the engine. Reese and I stepped back and Luke and Jimmy pulled away.

17

After Luke was gone, Reese told Steve and Dave that we wanted to walk them home. Reese was smiling so big now. She kept trying to slip her hand around Steve's arm, but he kept pulling away. He and Dave didn't like to be touched.

"We must go," said Steve. "We want to become familiar with the town."

"What's there to get familiar with? This street is basically it," said Reese.

They obviously didn't want to hang out with us anymore, and I tugged Reese away. As we left, Dave doubled up in pain again. I was standing closest, so I grabbed him, thinking he might fall. He didn't, but it made me feel good to help him. It made me feel warm and tingly and really happy. In fact, I had a slight problem letting go of him. I kept holding his arm and keeping my other hand on his back. It was so pleasant to touch him. I guess I liked him. And I guessed if Reese liked Steve, I could be with Dave.

Reese and I finally detached ourselves from them and walked home on the road. We were so happy and excited. We skipped around and danced and spun. Reese even fell on her butt at one point, and when I helped her up I noticed it didn't feel the same as when I helped Dave. It didn't have that same warm, tingly feeling. Reese said, "Wasn't it weird, how they had so much trouble walking?"

It was weird, but I couldn't think about that now. I was too busy looking at the stars and thinking how wonderful the universe was.

Back at my dad's house I was in the best mood. I went to the bathroom and looked at myself in the mirror and I looked so cute. I was tan and this zit that was next to my nose had cleared up. I just got it two days ago, so that was pretty good news. Also, my lips, which had been chapped, didn't look as chapped now. They looked round and cute and kinda sexy.

I went to see what my dad was doing. He was working on his computer. When he went to the kitchen to make tea, I noticed he wasn't limping at all. I asked him about it and he said it must be the weather. Or maybe the new medication he had tried was having a delayed effect.

The tea that night was so delicious. Also, I told my dad about how we had met these two guys and how cute they were and how smart. My dad didn't really approve.

He never liked hearing me talk about boys. But that was okay. I went to bed so I could be alone with my thoughts. I put on my pj's and got into bed. I put a CD on my little boom box to fall asleep, but I swear I didn't hear one note of it. The minute I put my head on my pillow I was out. I started dreaming and, oh my god, they were the best dreams! It was like I was floating on air and the sun was superclose to me and warming me and I was in a cloud that was all different colors and full of beautiful sounds that seemed to hum through my brain. Then these huge swirls of water were around me, bathing me in a warm glow of total happiness, and I somehow knew everything was okay and everyone loved everyone and the Earth was the best place in the entire galaxy. . . .

Part TWO

(Associated Press) NOVA SCOTIA. — U.S. Navy investigators continued to search for a lost Baldwin "Hellfire" missile in the North Atlantic. Violent seas and unusual storm patterns in the area have so far hindered recovery attempts.

The fully armed nuclear missile/torpedo hybrid was mistakenly fired from the submarine USS *Carlisle* during a training mission approximately three hundred miles south by southeast of Nova Scotia.

Canada's Maritime Council has petitioned the U.S. Navy for a full disclosure of all pertinent information regarding the location of the weapon and all possible risks to ocean life it may pose.

"If this nuclear device is leaking it could affect an area from Cape Cod to Greenland," said Walt Benjamin, spokesman for the CMC. "This could be the worst ecological disaster in the North Atlantic ever, and we need to know exactly what we are dealing with."

Initial Navy recovery efforts have been stymied by highly unusual summer storm activity in the area. "It is like the ocean itself is upset with us because of this unfortunate event," one Naval observer commented. The last such storm activity of this magnitude seen in the North Atlantic was recorded in 1907.

The International Weather Board confirmed the rareness of the storms but offered no explanation.

18

When I woke up the next morning I felt like I'd been asleep for years. Of course the minute my eyes opened I had one thought: *Where are Steve and Dave?* I had barely gotten dressed when my dad called to me, "Emily! Reese is here."

We didn't even think about eating breakfast. I threw on my clothes and grabbed my beach stuff and we walked down the road toward South Point.

"Oh my god!" I said as we hurried down the road. "I had the most amazing dreams last night!"

"I know, I know," said Reese, who seemed preoccupied.

"You had them, too?" I said. "With the sun and the water all around?"

She had. But she didn't seem very excited about them.

She seemed more worried. Also, we were walking so fast we were practically running.

"Wait," I said. "Why are we running?"

"I don't know," said Reese. She slowed down.

"What was up with those dreams?" I said.

Reese shook her head. "It's something about Dave and Steve. I know it is. Maybe it's a contact high."

"What's a contact high?"

"It's like if someone is on drugs, you get high, too, by being around them."

Reese knew more about drugs than I did, so I didn't feel qualified to say.

"And that would explain why they kept tripping over things and why they wouldn't eat," said Reese.

"You really think they were on drugs?"

"I don't know," said Reese a little testily. "It didn't seem like they were. But there has to be some explanation."

"I was hoping we'd see them again."

"I know. So was I."

We kept walking until we reached the beach. We found Nick and Justin and Sheila and some other people lying on their towels.

We spread out our own stuff and watched Nick and Justin throw a Frisbee. When Justin saw Reese he came over.

"What's up?" he said.

"Nothing," said Reese, ignoring him. To Sheila she said, "You haven't met two guys named Steve and Dave, have you?"

"No," said Sheila. "Who are they?"

"They're these two guys we hung out with last night," said Reese.

"Were they tan? And kinda hot?" asked Sheila.

"Very hot," said Reese. "They're in college. Or something. They studied in Germany."

"Oh no. The people I saw were speaking Spanish to a woman on the road."

"They might know Spanish," I said.

"Yeah," said Reese. "They're really smart."

"Do they kind of look like celebrities?" said Sheila.

"*Totally,*" said Reese excitedly. "Where did you see them?"

"I was walking our dog this morning. They were on the street talking to one of the women who works at our hotel."

"Are they staying there?" I asked.

"I don't know," said Sheila.

"They gotta be staying somewhere," said Reese.

"What kind of Spanish were they speaking?" I said. "Like were they trying to practice it?"

"Oh no," said Sheila. "They were fluent. I thought they were Spanish rock stars or something. One of them looked like Enrique Iglesias."

"What were they talking to a cleaning lady for, I wonder?" said Reese.

"Whatever it was, she was into it," said Sheila. "She had the biggest smile on her face. They must have been charming the pants off her. She was in love."

"I can speak Spanish," said Justin, who was getting jealous. He forced himself down between Reese and me.

Reese ignored him.

"*Como se llama,*" said Justin. "My namo is . . ."

"Your *namo* is *lamo,*" said Reese.

Justin frowned. "What's your problem?" he said seriously. "Why are you so into these German guys?"

"It's none of your business."

"I'll make it my business. I'll kick their German butts."

"They're not German."

"They're language students," I said.

"*Language students,*" scoffed Justin. "Who studies languages? Geeks."

"Hey, you guys," said Nick, coming over and flopping on a towel. "There's a party tonight. You should come. Do you know the Delancy house?"

We did. It was a huge old house that groups of college students rented.

"They're having a big bash," said Nick.

"Yeah, whatever," said Reese, looking up and down the beach for Steve and Dave.

I looked, too.

"I don't like the sound of these guys," said Justin, standing and flipping the Frisbee to one of the volleyball girls. "Geeks shouldn't come to the beach."

19

That night Reese and I ate dinner at her house. We were both quite depressed by the absence of Dave and Steve in our lives. We had also begun to separate the two of them between us. Like I would say how I loved Dave's dark eyes. Reese would say how she loved Steve's perfect skin. And of course we both loved how handsome and good-natured and well educated they were.

We ate with Reese's parents. Reese's dad, Mr. Ridgley, was a businessman from Boston. He did something with banks and made a lot of money. He didn't usually say much, but tonight he was chattering away. He told us about a conversation he had with the sheriff and how all these weird things were happening in town—not crimes exactly, but like people complaining about their dogs barking all night. Or strange people walking through people's backyards at odd times. And of course the weather had been very stormy, which was unusual for that time of year.

Mrs. Ridgley also had a strange occurrence to report. Mrs. Frohman, a coworker of hers at the Grace Church Thriftstore, had experienced a miraculous improvement in her arthritis. She was also hearing better. The weird part was that Mrs. Frohman kept insisting that both improvements had begun the day two strange boys had talked to her in the parking lot at the supermarket. They had helped her with her groceries and out of the blue they started speaking Hebrew to her, which she understood, because she was Jewish. She assumed they were Jewish boys or were tourists from Israel maybe, because they were tan and handsome and seemed a little out of place, like they weren't used to America. But once her hip started getting better she said it was a miracle and they were messengers from God. She was a little nutty anyway, but now she wouldn't shut up. She was driving everyone at the Thriftstore crazy.

"That sounds like Steve and Dave," I said.

Reese kicked me under the table. I glared at her.

"Who are Steve and Dave?" said Mr. Ridgley with interest.

"They're just these guys," said Reese. "They can't speak Hebrew, though."

"But who are they?" said Mr. Ridgley.

I started to speak, but Reese kicked me again. "They're just these guys," said Reese. "They're kind of annoying.

They go to Harvard and they show off how good they are at linguistics."

"Would they be the ones wandering around in people's yards?"

"No," said Reese. "They left anyway. They went back to Boston."

"Well, if they went to Harvard, I'm sure they're not the prowlers," said Mrs. Ridgley.

"We have to go to a party now," said Reese, wiping her face with her napkin. "We'll be gone for a while."

"Don't be out too late," said Mrs. Ridgley.

"And be careful," said Mr. Ridgley.

Outside, as we walked to the Delancy house, I asked Reese why she kept kicking me at dinner.

"Because you can't tell people about Steve and Dave."

"Why not?"

"Because people are going to find out. And something bad will happen."

"Find out what?"

"Just whatever. How weird they are. People freak out. Like your dad said. People get very touchy about things they don't understand."

"Yeah, but—"

"Trust me on this. I have hair on my arms and I'm Hairy Scary; what do you think people will say about them?"

"Yeah, but they're still just people. Right? I mean we don't have to lie to your dad."

"Lie to everyone. That's my philosophy," said Reese. She looked at her watch. "Do you think Steve and Dave might show up at the Delancy house?"

"I don't know," I said. "I sure hope so."

20

Reese and I had been to a party at the Delancy house the summer before. It had been pretty wild. There was a wet T-shirt contest and a lot of crazy frat boys running around.

That night we arrived early, though, so things were still relatively civilized. One of the guys who was renting it introduced himself. He studied computer stuff at U Mass. He was very sweet and gave us free cups for the keg. We walked around. There were DJs and dance music in the basement. In the backyard, tiki lamps were burning and people were flopped on old couches they had carried out from the house. We found the keg and waited in line to fill our cups.

That's when Harold and Carl and some of their crew showed up. They immediately insulted Reese with some comment about her Goth lipstick (she had dressed up for the party, including a dark, plum-colored lipstick and a heavy dose of black eyeliner). One of their friends asked us for a cigarette. We didn't have one. They wanted to crash in line with us to get beer and Reese made them go to the back of the line and warned everyone not to let them cut in front. That made them mad, but Reese didn't care.

Nick and Justin and Sheila appeared. I was so glad to see them. Nick came over and started talking to me, really shy and sweetlike; he was so awesome. Justin and Sheila, meanwhile, cut in line with Reese, which made the people behind us angry. It made Harold and Carl really angry, but when they started whining about it, Reese told them to "shut their pieholes."

Once we had beer, Nick and Justin wanted to check out the music. From the backyard we crept down the stone steps into the dark basement. It was very atmospheric down there. Floodlights shone on the brick walls in this spooky way. There was a big sound system with turntables and two DJs. They were big-city DJs, not like you would see at a school dance in Indianapolis. It was very groovy and "college" and I got a shiver of excitement all through me. Nick took my beer and set it on a little ledge so we could dance. He was very considerate like that. He led me in to the dancing people and we joined in.

Reese danced with Justin. It was very fun, and in a way, I was glad to be doing normal vacation stuff. The last two weeks had been kind of bizarre, beginning with the dead thing on the beach and then Luke almost shooting Jimmy and even meeting Steve and Dave, who were amazing but who seemed a little strange (what am I saying, *a lot* strange). So it was nice to dance with a boy I could like and who seemed to like me, and of course Reese would probably hook up with Justin again, and maybe Nick and Justin would be our boyfriends for the summer. That was what I really wanted: to have some normal fun. That's what summer was supposed to be about.

But then a strong sensation passed through me. It felt almost electric, my stomach felt watery, and my whole body turned to jelly for a moment, a warm, heavy jelly. I couldn't figure out what it was and I looked around and I saw two figures standing by the DJs. I couldn't see them because the light was behind them, but I knew it was Steve and Dave. I knew it before I could see them, almost like telepathy. I also knew they weren't just hanging out. They were there for a reason.

They were looking for us. They were looking for *me*.

21

At first Steve and Dave didn't do anything. They stood very still and watched people dance.

Reese didn't see them. She and Justin were dancing. I wasn't sure what to do, so I kept dancing. Finally I was getting too hot and I told Nick I was thirsty, but not for beer, and he immediately ran upstairs to get me a glass of water.

It was then that Reese saw Steve and Dave. She abandoned Justin and ran straight over to them. Reese was so excited she could barely contain herself. She led Steve and Dave toward the door and up the stone stairs, waving me along, too. Poor Justin just stood there, frozen in mid-dance. I wasn't sure what to do, either; I wanted to wait until Nick came back.

But I followed Reese. How could I resist Steve and Dave? Outside she grabbed them and started gushing. Where had they been? What had they done that day? Didn't they know we wanted to hang out?

Steve shrugged.

"You know, we heard something about you guys," said Reese.

"What?" said Steve.

"That you guys know Hebrew . . . and Spanish!"

Steve and Dave looked at her. They looked at me.

"Do you?" said Reese.

"We know . . . many languages," said Steve.

"How can you know that many, though?" said Reese. "I mean, I took Spanish for six years, and I can say a few things. Like *yo tengo frio* or whatever—"

"We know all languages," said Dave.

"—or like French words," continued Reese. "Like *voulez-vous couchez—*"

"Wait," I said. "You know *all* languages?"

Reese turned to Steve. "Say something in Chinese," she said, sipping her beer and grinning up at him like an idiot.

Steve and Dave ignored Reese. They focused on me. "We have to ask you something," Steve said.

But before they could, Dave suddenly doubled over with pain. I caught him. I struggled to hold him up. "Dave? Dave, are you all right?" I said.

Steve and Reese helped me straighten him up. Dave nodded that he was okay.

"Why don't you go to the hospital?" said Reese.

"You need to see a doctor," I said.

"Really," said Reese seriously. "What's wrong with you?"

"I just have pain," said Dave. "It is nothing."

"How can you say that?" said Reese. "You need to go to the emergency room."

"It's just pain," he said again. "It's normal."

"It's *not* normal," I said.

"I'm not in pain," said Reese. "Emily's not in pain."

Dave and Steve both looked at us. It was the strangest look. It seemed to say, *Oh, but you are.*

22

As we got Dave upright, someone tapped me on the shoulder. It was Nick. He had my glass of water. I pulled him into our group. He nodded politely to Dave and Steve. "I'm Nick," he said, holding out his hand to Steve.

Steve didn't shake it. At that moment, a loud noise came from the basement and the music suddenly stopped.

Everyone in the backyard looked toward the house. "The cops are here!" yelled a voice from inside.

"Luke Alert!" warned another voice.

"Doesn't he have anything better to do?" complained someone standing near us.

"What is happening?" asked Steve.

"Sounds like the cops are shutting down the party," Nick explained.

A bunch of partygoers crawled out of the basement and into the backyard. Some of the younger partiers quickly crawled over the wood fence at the back of the yard and disappeared into the woods.

"Busted!" shrieked a drunk girl on one of the couches. One of the DJs came out of the basement and lit a cigarette.

"Now what?" said Reese.

Nick stood close to me. In front of the house, on the street, a police siren squawked once. A police light began spinning, sending sharp red and blue lights around the neighborhood. There was a general groan from the dozen or so people standing in the yard. People hurried to finish their beers. A minute later, a light went on in the house. The police were coming inside; they were checking people's IDs.

There was also something happening on the third floor of the house. Two very young boys, probably twelve or thirteen, appeared at an open window. Reese saw them and pointed. Several people stopped what they were doing to watch them.

One of the boys stepped out of the window and began to walk along the rain gutter at the edge of the roof. The gutter did not look very sturdy. And he was three floors up.

"Dude!" said his friend, from the window. "What are you doing? That thing won't hold."

"Yes, it will. I've done it before," said the boy. He began

to make his way along the roof. There was a large tree at the opposite side of the house. If he reached it he was apparently going to climb down and thereby escape Deputy Luke and the police.

"Dude, it's not worth it," said his friend nervously from the window. "They can't bust us; we didn't do anything."

"I'm not hanging around to find out," said the boy. He was already halfway to the tree. It looked like he was going to make it.

A person down in the yard called up to the boys, "Hey, that gutter isn't very strong."

"I can't get in trouble," the boy walking the gutter said. "My dad will kill me." He was getting more cautious, though.

"The cops won't do anything," called another observer. "Go back. Don't risk it."

I could see the boy debating it in his head. On the one hand, Luke probably wouldn't do anything. On the other hand, he was only twenty feet from the tree, which, once he climbed down, would put him completely out of danger.

"I can make it," said the boy.

The seven or eight people still in the yard stared up at him. He proceeded slowly, step by step, leaning as much as he could on the steep roof, to avoid putting his full weight on the rickety rain gutter.

In the front of the house, another police car pulled up, Luke's uncle most likely. The South Point cops seemed to come down extra hard on the Delancy house. They understood that people came to South Point to party; they just didn't like it when the parties got too big or too concentrated. Or too young.

A few more partiers crawled over the back fence and ran into the woods, some of them giggling as they did. Above us, the kid on the roof was only ten feet from the tree.

Then there was a sickening groan. It sounded like a human voice, but in fact it was the metal of the rain gutter bending—and breaking. The kid slipped off the roof, fell, and somehow caught something so that his chest was level with the eaves of the roof. His legs swung helplessly in the air.

"Scottie! Help!" he cried to his friend.

His friend gasped in horror. He started to crawl out the window, then thought better of it. "Hang on!" he said, and he disappeared.

Everyone watched the kid. Reese clutched Steve's arm. I grabbed Nick. The kid swung silently in the air. Then the rain gutter bent more, broke more, and in total silence the kid suddenly released into the air, falling, turning slightly as he did, so that he was sideways when he landed in the stone stairwell that led to the basement. There was a soft *whump* sound when he hit.

People screamed. People ran toward the stairwell. Other people ran away from it. Reese, who loved gore, sprinted to it, followed closely by me, Steve, Nick, Dave. The five of us ran so fast we nearly knocked one another down the stairs. The body lay upside down on the bottom steps. The neck of the boy was twisted around in a terrible way. An older girl, wanting to help, ran down several steps toward the body. But when she saw what had happened to the boy's head and neck, she screamed and scrambled back out.

Steve pushed around the people and crept down the steps. He picked up the boy, which made more people scream, the people who hadn't realized the head was hanging off the body backward. Other people were saying not to touch the body. But that seemed pointless at this stage.

Steve turned to Reese and me. He spoke very clearly and with great authority. He said, "I'm going to take this boy into the basement. I'm going to shut this door. I need you to keep everyone out for three minutes. Can you do that?"

We looked at him in utter shock.

"Can you do that?" he repeated.

"Yes," sputtered Reese. "We can do that."

23

Steve took the body into the dark basement and shut the door. I swear, my heart was pounding so hard. A girl I didn't know ran down to the door, I guess to stop Steve, but Nick caught her by the waist and dragged her back. Dave held her, too, and the minute he touched her, she gave up struggling and looked at Dave in a strange way.

People began backing away from the stairwell. They began running away. They ran to the back of the yard and climbed over the fence.

Luke appeared on the back porch. Jimmy stood behind him. They could see people were crawling over the fence, but Jimmy and Luke didn't seem to care. Instead they shone their flashlights around the backyard. "Any of you the renters of this residence?" asked Luke calmly.

No one answered.

"Reese, Emily," said Luke, shining his light into our faces. "I should have known you two would be here."

"We're not doing anything," said Reese, trying to be her usual defiant self but sounding more scared than anything.

Luke sensed something was up. "What's going on down there? Is that the basement?"

"Nothing's going on," said Reese. I thought about the three minutes. There was no way we were going to keep Luke out of the basement.

Luke came onto the lawn. He approached the top of the stone stairwell. He aimed his flashlight down the steps. I thought I saw a tiny patch of blood on one of the lower steps, but Luke didn't see it.

"Anyone want to tell me what's going on here?" said Luke again.

"Nothing," said Nick, jamming his hands guiltily into his jeans.

"Nothing?" said Luke. "Then why are you all standing here looking scared to death?"

No one spoke.

Luke glanced back at Jimmy, who was still on the porch. "Maybe that's where the keg is," suggested Jimmy.

"No," said Luke, "because the keg is over there." He pointed his flashlight into the yard and found the silver metal of the keg, which was partially hidden behind a beach chair.

Luke returned his attention to the stairwell. He made another sweep with his flashlight of the door and the lower steps. Again he missed the blood spot. Jimmy came down from the porch. Jimmy, I noticed, no longer carried a gun.

Luke went down a couple steps. He turned on his shoulder radio and told his dispatcher where he was. Then he saw the blood. He kept his light on it and reached down and touched it. "Jesus," he muttered to himself. He turned on us. "Goddammit, you guys, this isn't funny! Tell me what's going on here!"

No one spoke.

"I'm serious; what is this? What the hell happened here?"

No one said a word.

Luke tried the door. It was locked. He clicked on his radio again. "Uncle Will, I've got some blood down here on the basement steps. And the door's locked. I'm going in."

Luke had some trouble getting his gun out of his holster, since he had his flashlight and radio already in hand. When he had everything ready, he pounded on the door. "This is the deputy sheriff! Open this door!" he yelled. There was no response. He tried the door again. The lock held. He stepped back and kicked the door. Nothing happened. Jimmy went down the steps to help. The two of them kicked again; the door gave slightly. They kicked a third time and the door slammed violently open. Luke held it open with his hand and picked up his flashlight. He stuck his head inside. *How much time has gone by?* I wondered.

Luke stepped forward. For a horrifying moment he disappeared into the darkness. There was silence for several seconds, then a sound like someone tripping over something; then Luke began cursing loudly. Finally

Luke's angry voice rang out: "What the hell are *you* doing down here?"

A second later Luke reappeared, holding the young boy roughly by his upper arm. The boy was delirious, wobbly, asleep looking. But he was alive. His head was on straight. He was no longer mangled. He was no longer . . . *dead.*

"Get up the stairs!" Luke ordered him. "You little brat . . ."

The boy could barely walk, so Luke dragged him up the stairs. Luke was very angry. At the top of the stairs he threw the boy down on the grass. "This kid is dead drunk!" he yelled at us. "Who is giving a kid this age alcohol? Huh? Who? Which one of you is responsible for this!"

No one spoke.

"I'm taking you all in," Luke said, flashing his light around at us. "Every last one of you. This is not funny! This is not funny *at all!*"

24

But before Luke could act, a soft popping sound came from the darkness of the basement. Luke spun around, refocused his flashlight on the basement door. A puff of black smoke appeared and a steady stream of it drifted out of the stairwell.

"Christ!" he said. He turned his flashlight beam back into the darkness. He gripped his radio: "Uncle Will. Everyone. I gotta fire now. I'm gonna need some fire extinguishers—"

Jimmy ran back into the house and appeared a second later with a fire extinguisher from the kitchen. A minute later, two more deputies appeared with extinguishers from their police cars. They all ran into the basement.

Dave grabbed my arm. He grabbed Reese, too, and

pulled us away. We retreated to the wood fence at the back of the yard. But faced with such an obstacle, Dave stopped. He did not seem to know how to climb a fence.

Nick seemed to understand the problem and with one strong kick knocked one of the boards out. We all scrambled through. Much to my relief, Steve suddenly appeared. He had slipped out of the basement somehow. He helped everyone through the fence.

We ran along a path, or what we thought was a path. It went for about fifty yards and sort of fizzled out. We were far enough from the house to be safe for the moment, but now we were lost in the woods.

Steve and Dave were leading the way now. Dave made a sound. It was a strange croaking sound, like you might make if you had allergies and your throat itched. And then, I swear to god, a bunch of frogs croaked, all in unison. It was the craziest thing. And suddenly Dave knew where to go. Also, after we'd stumbled along for a while, a bunch of birds began chattering above us, which was weird that late at night. Weren't birds usually asleep? Reese was noticing this stuff, too. And I guess Nick must have also. We were all looking around like "what the—?" But no one said anything. We were too busy tripping and falling and crashing through the brush.

Steve and Dave continued to lead. I had no idea where we were going, but they did. Suddenly we were at the highway by the beach. We ran across the road and ducked out of sight, barely avoiding a fire truck as it sped by. We hid in the bushes by the highway, the five of us, Nick and me, Reese, Dave, and Steve. We were all breathing hard. Steve and Dave were especially breathing hard.

They seemed freaked out by our run through the woods. They kept looking at themselves, at their cuts and scrapes. They seemed shocked they were bleeding, that parts of their bodies were actually injured. It was like they had never done anything like that before. They were so weird.

Then I remembered that Steve had just brought someone back from the dead. Had that really happened? *That* was weird. That was beyond weird. I tried not to think about it. I tried to think about the beach and how tomorrow we would go to the beach and swim and hang out like we always did. All this other stuff. It was too much. It was a dream. It had to be. But Steve reached over and touched my arm. "Your father," he said. "Where is he? We must go to him. We must speak to your father."

I stared back into his strange face. I looked at his hand where it touched my arm. I realized then that I was going to help him. I had no choice.

25

Once we'd all caught our breath, the five of us walked to the beach and began walking toward my house. We tried to stay near the dunes, where it would be harder to see us from the road, in case the police were looking for us. Unfortunately, the sand was drier and looser and harder to walk on. We hadn't gone a half mile or so when Dave flopped down on the sand, breathing heavily. He was totally exhausted. The rest of us flopped down as well.

Nick was the only one who didn't. He continued to stand. He seemed upset. He was shaking his head slightly, staring at the ocean. He turned to Dave and Steve. "Listen . . . ," he finally said. "I'm sorry, but I just gotta ask you, what on earth just happened back there?"

Dave and Steve didn't answer.

"I'm serious," said Nick. "That kid. I'm not saying you did anything wrong. But what did you do to him?"

"We helped him," said Steve.

"Yeah, but how? What did you do?"

"We . . . ," said Steve, unsure of how to explain.

"No," said Nick. "Not *we*. You. Steve. You did something. What was it? That kid's neck . . ."

"We have very special training," said Steve.

"We are . . . different . . . ," said Dave.

"Yeah, *obviously*," said Nick.

"Yeah," said Reese, joining in. "You did something. That boy did not look good."

"That boy was *dead*," said Nick.

"He was very badly injured," said Steve.

"What did you do?" said Nick. "Tell us."

"Well . . . ," said Steve.

We all stared at him.

He hesitated. He started again: "Do you know how . . . a magnet can make metal shavings change shape? It can make metal shavings realign themselves, in patterns?"

"Yeah?" said Nick. "So?"

"Well, cells, in your body, they have electricity in them. And they align in certain ways. And if the alignment is not correct, the presence of a powerful magnet . . ."

"Yeah, okay," said Nick. "But where's the magnet?"

"We have techniques that can influence cells," said Dave; his eyes were closed and he was still breathing hard. "We can bring them into harmony."

Nick stared at him. He shook his head. "Dudes, I'm

not trying to be a jerk here. You just took a kid whose head was bent around *backward—*"

"My dad!" I said suddenly. "Something happened to him, too. His hip got better. He doesn't limp anymore!"

Dave and Steve looked intently at each other. "Your father," Dave said to me. "He had contact with the organism on the beach?"

"You know about that?" said Reese. "The sparkly blob thing?"

"My dad was there," I said. "We tried to go down, too, but they wouldn't let us."

"You saw it?" said Dave.

"Of course we saw it," said Reese.

"Where is it now?" said Steve with a new urgency.

"We don't know," I said. "They took it somewhere."

"But your father knows," said Steve, staring at me.

"He might have an idea," I said. "But I think it's a secret. The government has it."

"Your father will tell us," said Dave. He got up. But he staggered and almost fell. Nick and I caught him and held him up. The minute I touched him, that same warm, tingly feeling came into me. Nick felt it, too; I could see it in his face. It shocked him, just like it shocked me the first time. It kind of filled you up somehow. It filled you with warmth and happiness. But Nick didn't trust it. You could see it in his face; he released Dave and stared at him. All of this was too much. It was too hard to take. I felt the same way.

I guess we all did.

26

At the end of the beach, we went to my house. It was now almost midnight; my dad would probably be worried and waiting for me. As we approached, I could see the light in the living room. There was my dad, with his reading glasses on, hard at work on his computer. We went to the door. I knocked once, so as not to scare him, then I opened the door, and we went inside.

We must have looked pretty ragged. We were scraped up and muddy and covered with sand.

My dad looked at us from his computer. At first he kept working, but when all of us had entered he stopped. He lifted his reading glasses off his face. He squinted to see who exactly was there.

"Hi, Dad," I said.

"Emily," he said back. He got up. He came over.

"These are my friends. This is Nick. And this is Steve and Dave."

My dad came forward. "Nice to meet you," he said.

"Professor Dalton, it is good to meet you," said Steve.

"Oh, you know my name," said my dad cheerfully. "What are your last names?"

Steve and Dave did not speak. Nick said, "Nick Garrison."

"And yours?" my dad said to Dave and Steve.

They looked at each other. "Smith," said Steve.

"Steve and Dave Smith?" said my dad.

"I thought you said you weren't brothers?" said Reese.

"My name is Smith," said Steve. "His name is Williams."

"I see," said my father. He was watching them now very closely. I thought he suspected they had made up their names. But I saw he was studying them in a different way. He was looking at their skin and their hair. My dad is a very observant person. He knew *instantly* there was something weird about them.

I spoke up. "We just wanted to have a cup of tea, if that's okay," I said. "We were at a party."

"Yeah," said Reese. "And this kid fell off the roof—" But she stopped.

"There was a fire," I said, covering for her. "Not a bad one, but Luke and the sheriff had to come."

"The sheriff?" said my father, who was staring at Dave.

"I'll go start the tea," I said. I went to the kitchen and

put water on the stove. Reese came in with me. She gave me a wild look like, *Now what are we going to do?*

Nick came into the kitchen, too, and stood with us, sneaking looks through the doorway at my dad and Dave and Steve.

I peeked out, too. Just then, Dave had one of his stomach cramps and my dad asked him what was wrong and Steve said Dave had trouble with his digestion.

"Really?" said my dad, helping him sit on the couch. "What kind of diet do you have?"

Dave and Steve couldn't think of an answer.

My dad watched them. I have never seen his eyes so alert in all my life. He was totally focused on Dave and Steve. It was intense. People had always told me my dad was a brilliant scientist, but all I ever saw him do was smoke his pipe and complain if I didn't get home on time. Now I was seeing the thing I'd always heard about. I was seeing a very smart person faced with a very interesting and complicated situation.

Suddenly Reese grabbed my arm. She pointed out the back window. Nick saw it, too. Two police cars were coming down our road. Their overhead lights were on and they were coming fast.

27

I ran into the living room. "The sheriff's coming," I said.

Steve pulled Dave off the couch. "They cannot find us," Steve told my dad. "I hope you understand."

My dad didn't argue. But then Dave almost fell and my father had to help steady him. When my father touched Dave he got the warm, tingly feeling. I could see it in his face.

"Where can we go?" said Steve.

My father was still registering the effect of touching Dave. For a moment he did nothing but slowly pull his hand back and look at his fingers.

"We can all go upstairs," I said. "To the attic."

I helped Dave from one side; Steve helped him from the other. We hurried into the hall and up the tiny stairs into the attic. Reese and Nick were behind us. They shoved our butts to make us go faster. Steve and I pushed open the trapdoor and we all scrambled upward through the dark opening. Then we spread out on the attic floor and stayed as quiet as we possibly could.

I could hear the knock at the front door. My dad opened it. Since the attic was over the living room we could hear everything.

"Sheriff Moshofsky," said my dad. "Hello, nice to see you."

"How are you this evening, Professor?"

"I'm good. Oh, hello, Luke. Jimmy. What brings you all out tonight?"

"Is your daughter home?" said the sheriff.

"I think she and Reese went to a party," said my dad. "It's getting kind of late actually . . . oh my, it's quarter past twelve. They're not in some kind of trouble, are they?"

"Not exactly. They were at a party at the Delancy house earlier this evening."

"Was there a problem?"

"We've got conflicting reports," said the sheriff. "My nephew here seems to think—"

"It wasn't just me," Luke said. "We have witnesses."

"Witnesses to what?" said my father.

The sheriff spoke in a deap voice: "We found a twelve-year-old boy who was severely intoxicated. And I mean severely."

Luke interrupted: "He fell out a three-story window. We thought he was drunk, but we gave him a Breathalyzer and it came up negative."

The sheriff: "He was probably on drugs, maybe some kind of designer drug."

"This kid didn't know what planet he was on," said Luke.

"There was also a fire," interrupted the sheriff. "The point is, we've got something of a mess and people are already jumpy anyway. You know, we've had these prowler reports. . . ."

"I see," said my dad.

"There were two men there tonight," said Luke. "They were with Emily and Reese last night. We think they're involved."

"We just want to talk to everyone who was there," said the sheriff. "Including your daughter."

"Some strange goings-on," said my dad sympathetically. He had always liked the sheriff.

"When do you expect your daughter will be home?"

"You know," said my father, "she sleeps over at Reese's house quite a bit. She could be there. She usually calls, though. Or they might be walking back on the beach."

There was a pause and the sheriff said, "When she shows up could you give us a call?"

"Absolutely," said my dad.

"Good night, Professor," said Luke.

"Good night," said my dad.

I crept to the attic window and watched while Jimmy, Luke, and his uncle got in their respective police cars. I watched them pull onto the road. They turned left. They were going to Reese's house.

28

We came down the stairs. My dad stood in the living room with his hands on his hips. He was thinking. When the five of us came into the room he frowned slightly.

Nick tugged on my arm. "I have to go," he whispered to me. "My parents will be wondering where I am."

"Okay," I said. I glanced at Steve and Dave to see how they would react. But they seemed fine with Nick leaving.

Nick went to the door and I walked him outside and onto the lawn.

"Nick?" I said.

"Yeah?"

"You won't tell anybody, right? About all this. It seems like we should probably keep it a secret."

"Yeah, I guess. Who would believe it anyway?"

"I know," I said. I walked closer to him. He seemed embarrassed and humbled by everything that had happened. "You know, if things were normal," I said, "I was hoping you and I would hang out tonight."

"Yeah?"

"Did you?" I asked.

He hesitated, then nodded. "Yeah," he said. "But things are so not normal."

"But maybe they will be."

"I don't know," he said. "It kind of doesn't feel that way."

We stopped and faced each other. He didn't speak, so I stepped closer and kissed him on the cheek. He still looked embarrassed, but he smiled at least. He leaned forward and kissed me on the mouth. It didn't last long, but it was slow and careful and he seemed to really mean it. I lingered as long as I could. But he had to leave, and I had to get back inside.

"Okay," he said, pulling away. He walked backward a few steps, waved, then began a slow jog down the road.

In the house, my father had Steve and Dave sitting at the kitchen table. They had steaming cups of tea in front of them. There was a plate of cookies in the middle of the table. Reese, sitting at one end of the table, was slurping her tea noisily. She was eating cookies as fast as she could get them. I immediately ate three myself. We hadn't eaten all night.

My father sipped his tea. Steve smelled his tea. Dave sat without moving. He hadn't even touched his cup.

"You don't like tea?" my dad asked Steve.

"No," said Steve. "Not really."

My dad watched him. "You've had tea before, though?"

"Yes," said Steve, "Of course. I just . . ."

Steve was a terrible liar.

My dad turned his attention to Dave, who was staring into his cup like he'd never seen tea before. My dad was figuring something out. My dad is so smart.

Steve picked up his cup. He touched it to his lips but was afraid of it somehow. He put it down. "It's very hot."

"You're not eating the cookies, either," observed my dad, more to himself than to us.

Steve and Dave looked at their plates. "You have to excuse us," said Steve vaguely.

"Is there something I could get you?" my dad asked.

"No," said Steve. "What we need to speak to you about is the organism on the beach. You were there when they found it?"

"Yes."

"Where did they take it?" asked Steve.

My dad studied him for a moment, obviously debating what to tell these two strangers. He decided to tell them the truth. "Originally it went to the Coast Guard base in Crutchfield," said my dad. "I'm guessing it will be moved. If it hasn't been already."

Steve said nothing. Dave touched the hot mug with his fingertips.

"Are you sure I can't make you something to eat?" asked my dad. "I have juice, too. Surely you want something to drink. Water? Purified water? You must be thirsty."

"No, thank you," said Steve. "Why would they move the organism?"

"Because they don't know what it is," said my dad simply. "Because they've never seen anything remotely like it before."

"What will they do with it?"

"Nothing, hopefully," said my dad. "Study it. They will be cautious . . . at first."

"Where might they take it?"

"There are several possibilities. It would depend on who's involved."

Steve nodded.

My father gripped his own teacup. "Can I ask *you* a question?"

"Of course," said Steve.

"Where did it come from? The organism, I mean?"

Steve and Dave looked at each other. They shrugged. Or I should say, they tried to shrug; it was one of those things they didn't seem to know how to do.

"That's nothing, Professor," said Reese suddenly. "That kid the sheriff was talking about. His neck was broken. I swear to god it was. And they fixed it." She pointed at Steve. "They took him in the basement and brought him back to life."

"And your hip got better," I said to my dad. "After you touched the thing on the beach. They can heal things. They do it by magnets or cells or whatever."

My dad watched me while I spoke. He turned to Steve. "So you're related in some way to the organism on the beach?"

Steve slowly moved his head up and down.

My father watched them closely. "I see. Well, this is very interesting. Yes, this is very interesting indeed."

29

My dad didn't get any more questions answered, not right then anyway. Luke, Jimmy, and Sheriff Moshofsky were back. They were coming up the front stairs. Reese saw them and sounded the alarm.

We didn't have time to get to the attic. So we ran Steve and Dave into my bedroom. Reese and I pushed them into my closet and climbed out the window. That was my idea. We had to show our faces at some point. If we could get outside, we could pretend to be coming home from the beach.

We crept around to the side of the house and watched while my dad welcomed them in again. This time they seemed a lot more serious. The three of them stood in the middle of the living room. The sheriff and

Jimmy stood close to my dad, and I saw Luke try to glance at the papers on my father's desk. Reese and I stayed hidden and listened through the open window.

"There's no sign of them at the Ridgleys'," said the sheriff. "And now Mr. Ridgley is very upset. I don't know what's going on, but whatever it is, we need to get it sorted out."

"I'm sorry," said my dad. "I don't know where they are."

"Well, they've got to be somewhere," said the sheriff. "Nobody's on the beach. Nobody's on the road. Are you sure you're being straight with us, Professor? I mean, there are no real crimes here. Nobody's in real trouble. But if people keep acting strangely, well, that tends to suggest there is more here than meets the eye."

I elbowed Reese. It was time for us to appear. We stood up and as naturally as we could walked to the front door and opened it.

The sheriff stopped talking to look at us. We had been in the dark, so we blinked in the brightness just as if we'd walked home from somewhere.

"Well, look who's here," said Luke.

They sat us down on the couch. The sheriff started the questioning. Reese did her usual defiant act. I tried to answer the questions and keep the story straight.

Sheriff: "When did you leave the party?"

Me: "When the fire started. We got scared. We thought we might get in trouble."

Sheriff: "Who started the fire?"

Me: "We don't know."

Sheriff: "Were those exchange students at the party?"

Me: "Yes."

Sheriff: "Did they start the fire?"

Me: "They couldn't have; they were outside with us."

Sheriff: "What about the one who went in the basement?"

Me: "Which one was in the basement?"

Sheriff: "The taller one. The one called Steve."

Me: "I don't remember."

"Oh, cut the crap," interrupted Luke. "You know they were in there and you know where they are now!"

I shook my head. It was weird. I was not a good liar usually. I never lied. But I seemed utterly capable of it now. "I don't know where anyone is," I said.

"What drugs was that twelve-year-old kid on?" said Luke.

I shook my head and shrugged.

Sheriff Moshofsky slapped his little notebook shut. He was upset now. "I don't like this," he told my dad. "I don't know what this is, some sort of prank you all are playing, but I'd be very careful if I were you."

"Uncle Will," said Luke. "Look!" He nodded his head toward the dining-room table. There were five teacups on it. Luke stepped forward and touched one. "Still warm," he said.

Sheriff Moshofsky immediately stood up.

Jimmy grabbed for his gun, but he didn't have one.

"Jesus, they're right here," whispered the sheriff. He drew his gun and looked at the ceiling and around the room.

Luke pointed his flashlight down the hallway toward the bedrooms. He reached for his own gun.

"No," said the sheriff. "Put that away." Luke put his gun back in its holster.

"Professor," said the sheriff, still listening carefully for any sound or movement. "At this time I would like to request permission to search the premises."

"Well, I . . . ," said my dad. "I don't know what the procedure—"

There was a noise from the back of the house.

"I'll take that as a yes," said the sheriff.

Luke charged down the hall toward the two bedrooms. We all ran to watch. He went for my dad's room first. Luke crashed through the door and went barreling in, his flashlight up, ready to hit someone.

It was empty.

The sheriff, who was right behind him, turned to my room. He tried the doorknob, found it unlocked, and pushed it open. "South Point Police!" he called out, ducking to the side. Then he stepped forward, leveling his gun and pointing it around the room. Reese and I both cringed and held our ears.

But there was nothing there. The bedroom was empty. The closet was empty. The curtain fluttered in the breeze at my open window.

Part THREE

(Associated Press) WASHINGTON, D.C. — Several environmental groups and the Canadian Maritime Council have filed a joint lawsuit in U.S. Federal Court today in an attempt to force the U.S. Navy to release classified documents regarding a missing Baldwin "Hellfire" missile that is believed to be leaking deadly radioactivity in an undisclosed location in the North Atlantic.

The fully armed tactical nuclear torpedo was mistakenly fired from the submarine USS *Carlisle* during a training mission approximately three hundred miles southeast of Nova Scotia. It was lost at sea and has not been recovered.

"Fishermen are finding species of sea life in their nets that we have literally never seen before," said a spokesman from Canada's Green Alliance. "This leads us to believe that this missile is probably at the bottom of MacKenzie's Crevice, an underwater canyon that is thought to be the deepest point in the Atlantic Ocean. If that is the case, it is doing untold damage to an ecosystem that has never been studied and is largely unknown."

A spokesman for the Navy expressed his regrets about the incident but cited national security as the primary reason for the lack of disclosure. "We obviously regret the damage to the sea life in the area and continue with our recovery efforts in hopes of minimizing that damage. Unfortunately, there are places in this part of the ocean that are deeper than our submersible technology can function at this time. You can't retrieve something if you can't get to where it is."

A scientists at the Halifax Marine Institute was quoted as saying: "This isn't the ideal way to get our first look at some of these deep-sea life-forms, but we are taking the opportunity to study them anyway. It's truly an astounding range of organic material we are finding."

30

I slept in a fever that night. I was so freaked out. I had the same dreams of sun and water, but they didn't have the same comfortable warm feeling. Then I had nightmares. At one point I saw my dad; something bad was happening, and he was standing in the road, and Reese and I were calling to him and waving for him to come. He wouldn't move; he didn't seem to hear us; he just stood there looking old and confused.

I called Reese. She didn't have a good night, either. When she got home she tried to sneak upstairs and her parents caught her. They were totally pissed. Reese's parents never got mad about stuff like staying out. I guess they were scared because the sheriff came over. They even grounded her, which was a first for Reese. Her parents never did things like that.

But these were small matters. "Did you have the dreams?" I asked.

"A little," said Reese. "Not like the first time."

"I had nightmares. About my dad."

"I know; I had weird dreams this morning. We have to find Steve and Dave, though. What if they're in trouble?"

"I wonder where they went?" I said.

"Do you think the sheriff could have found them?"

"I doubt it," I said.

"What did your dad say about them?" asked Reese.

"I don't know, I haven't talked to him yet. I'm afraid to get out of bed."

"I know; me, too," said Reese. "This is turning out to be such a weird summer."

Neither of us talked. I could hear birds outside chirping. I wondered what they were saying.

"You know what?" I said. "We should go to the beach. That's what we should do. None of this is our fault."

"You're right," agreed Reese. "It's not like we did anything wrong."

"We didn't do anything."

"Let the sheriff worry about things," said Reese. "That's what they get paid for."

"God, I wonder where Steve and Dave are, though?" I said.

"I know," said Reese. "I just want to lie here and think about them."

"And dream those dreams," I said. "Those are the best dreams."

"They are. They're better than being in love."

Finally, I put on my bathrobe and went into the living room. My dad was just coming in. He was wearing a coat. He had driven somewhere.

"Hello, Emily," he said.

"Good morning," I said back. He didn't seem to be mad. Why should he be?

"Where have you been?" I asked.

"I went to see if I could get a DNA reading off the teacups your friends were drinking from last night."

"DNA reading?"

"DNA, or cellular tissue, or fingerprints. Anything we can get. I dropped the cups off with an old colleague of mine."

"What do you think he'll find out?"

"I don't know, honey."

I sat down at the table. "Dad, are you mad?"

"No. Why would I be mad?" He pulled out his pipe and slapped it against his hand like he does.

"Reese's parents grounded her."

"For what?"

I shrugged. "Staying out too late, I guess. And because everyone's getting so paranoid."

"I'm not mad," said my dad. "I'm very concerned for those young men, though. I think they may have sought you out, and me, because we had contact with the organism on Hadley Beach."

"Really? You think Steve and Dave have something to do with that?"

"They certainly were interested in it." He stuffed his pipe. "I'm trying to get access to see it again. The little bits of information I'm getting are too extraordinary to believe. I'm going to drive down to Crutchfield tomorrow."

"Are you going to tell Steve and Dave where it is?"

"I don't know. I don't know exactly what their intentions are."

"They're not trying to hurt anyone," I said. "They saved that boy. And I think they saved Jimmy that night he got shot. So they're not bad."

"Yes, well, let's hope not."

I watched him clean his pipe. "Did you notice what happens when you touch them?"

"I did," he said quietly.

"It's like a little warm feeling spreads all through you."

"It's some sort of electrochemical transmission . . . ," said my dad.

"Did you have the dreams?"

"The dreams?" He looked up from his pipe. "You've had them, too?"

I nodded. "Since the first time we met them. Both Reese and I have had them every night."

"You both . . . ?" My father shook his head. "This is too incredible to believe."

"Where do you think Steve and Dave came from?" I asked.

"It would be pointless to speculate . . . ," he said. He got up and walked across the room. He stood over his computer thinking. "For some reason, as unlikely as it sounds, I think they came from the ocean."

"But they're human; how could they breathe?"

"They are definitely human now. But they're not very good at it. They can't eat. They can't drink. The short one, Dave, is in constant pain. No, my guess is that this is not their natural state. They have become human because they want something. And they need to get it quickly. They are not going to survive very long."

"But if they're not human, what are they? And how did they get in the ocean?"

My dad sighed. "That is the most interesting question of all."

31

I went over to Reese's after that. Her parents weren't very good disciplinarians. She was supposed to be grounded, but her mom went to work at the Grace Church Thrift-store and her dad was in Boston at a meeting. So no one was there to enforce it.

Reese decided to go to the beach.

"Reese, you're grounded," I said.

"So?" said Reese. "The beach is on the ground."

So we went. We walked down the road. We had our flip-flops and our sunglasses and our L.L. Bean beach bags, but we weren't in a good mood. We were tired and frowning, even though the sun was out and the sky was perfectly blue. Neither of us said it, but Steve and Dave were all we could think about.

At Antonio's we had $2.99 specials, not the best breakfast. Then we slogged through the sand to the beach.

We felt better, though, when we saw Nick and Justin and Sheila lying on their towels in the sun. I guess Nick had told the others what happened, because they stared at us when we first arrived. No one wanted to say anything.

Sheila finally scooted over to me. "Are you guys okay?" she whispered to me.

I nodded. "Not really, though," I said.

"Nick told us what happened. That is *soo* scary."

"I know. And now we don't even know where Steve and Dave are, or what happened."

"Do you think they work for the CIA?" said Sheila.

"No," I said.

"Who do you think they are?" she asked.

I was going to repeat what my dad said, that they came from the ocean. But I thought of what Reese said: people freak out about things they don't understand.

"I'm not sure," I said. "I just want to have fun anyway. I don't want it to ruin my whole summer."

"No, I think you're right," said Sheila. "Having the police come to your house, that sucks."

I agreed. I lay on my towel and closed my eyes.

After a while Justin and Nick wanted us to come in the water with them. Nick and I swam way out and bobbed around in the surf.

"How are you doing?" he asked.

"I'm okay, I guess. How are you doing?"

"All right," he said. "That was the weirdest night of my life last night."

"We probably shouldn't tell people stuff," I said.

"Yeah?"

"Don't you think?" I said. I was treading water. "Because people can't deal with it."

"Maybe you're right."

"Can I tell you something weird?"

"Sure."

"My dad thinks they're from the ocean."

"The ocean? Really? *This* ocean?" said Nick, glancing down at the water.

I hadn't thought of that. I looked down, too. But you couldn't see anything. You couldn't even see your own legs.

Nick sort of panicked and started swimming back toward shore. I did, too. But when we got closer to shore, we calmed down. It was too nice to get out completely. The water felt clean and fresh and fizzy in this pleasant way.

"Did you have the dreams?" I asked Nick.

"What dreams?"

"The dreams of water and the sun."

"I don't know," he said. "I dreamed of you, though."

"Really?" I said. "Like what?"

"Just that I was with you."

"Oh," I said.

"I mean, not like anything in particular. Just hanging out."

"Oh," I said again.

When we returned to our towels everyone put sunscreen on one another. Nick did me. He spent a lot of time rubbing my back and my neck. He was being really gentle and kind. Everyone was being really nice to one another. We were under a lot of stress.

32

That night Nick, Justin, Sheila, Reese, and I went to Antonio's. We all had specials with large Cokes; everyone was thirsty from being in the sun all day. Two of the volleyball girls showed up and said there was a party on the beach. It was a beautiful night, so that made sense. Still, Nick and Reese and I hesitated. We'd had enough late-night adventures to last us all summer. But Sheila and Justin wanted to go. They were mad that they'd missed all the excitement. So we went.

It was a little spooky walking over the dunes in the dark. Once we found the party and met the people we felt better. They had a big fire and marshmallows and one of them was playing an acoustic guitar. Justin immediately went over to Reese and she let him put his arm around her. I was wondering what Nick would do. One of the volleyball girls kept talking to him. But when people finally settled around the fire he came over and sat with me.

I snuggled up next to him. Usually I would be too shy, but I needed comforting at that point. Nick put his arm around me and pulled me close and kissed me once on the forehead. I closed my eyes and let my head rest on his chest and everything felt okay again. It felt so good, it was almost like the dreams, except it was real, and it was Nick. So in a way, it was better.

Then, *yuck,* Harold and Carl showed up. They were walking down the beach and Harold came over. He saw Reese and stood over her. "Hey, *Reese,*" he said with that snotty sound in his voice.

"What do you want, *Harold?*" sneered Reese. She was sitting with her arms around her knees; Justin was next to her.

"Did you hear about your friends?"

Reese stared up at him. I instantly sat up.

"What about them?" said Reese.

"They're going after them. The sheriff has a warrant for their arrest."

"Dave and Steve?" I said. "But why? What did they do?"

"They didn't do anything. It's that kid from the party, who fell off the roof. He has memory damage. He can't remember anything. He can't remember his own name. So his parents are suing."

"Who are they suing?" said Nick.

"Everyone. The cops. Your friends."

"But Steve and Dave were only trying to help," said Nick.

"Well, that's what happens when you try to help." Harold laughed. "You get sued!"

"Yeah, but getting sued doesn't mean they can arrest them," said Sheila.

"Sure they can. For arson. They started the fire."

"They can't prove that," said Reese.

"They don't have to," said Harold. "This isn't Boston. In this town, if the sheriff wants you, he gets you." He stood there, grinning down at us.

"That's crap," said Reese. "You don't know what you're talking about."

"The sheriff isn't like that anyway," I said. This was true. Sheriff Moshofsky wasn't some redneck cop who harassed people.

"Yeah, but maybe it's not just the sheriff anymore," said Harold. "Did you ever think of that? Maybe it's coming from higher up the chain of command."

33

After the beach party, Nick, Justin, and Sheila returned to their hotel. Reese and I walked up and down the deserted main street a couple times before we went home. I don't know what we were hoping for exactly; I guess that Steve and Dave would appear, or that Luke would drive by and we could explain what really happened at the Delancy house.

But nothing happened. The crickets chirped. The stars moved across the sky. We headed home. Reese walked me to my house. From my front yard we could see my dad inside working on his computer while he talked on the phone. He looked very excited. Reese decided to come inside.

"Dad?" I said as we entered.

He was busy, though. He was talking on the phone in a very excited voice. I had explained to Reese that my dad had done tests on the teacups Dave and Steve had drunk from. So she was as curious as I was.

"Dad?" I said when he seemed to be waiting for someone on the other end.

But he wasn't paying attention. You could see his brain working.

"Dad?" I said a third time.

"Yes, honey, what is it?"

"Did your friend do the tests?"

"Yes, he did the tests."

"And what did they say?"

He took a deep breath. "The tests are very interesting. We're looking into them."

"Are Dave and Steve normal humans?" I asked.

"They have human cells," said my dad. "So technically yes. But their cells do odd things. They don't act like human cells."

"What does that mean?"

"Hello?" he said into the phone. "No, I'm still here. . . . No, I can wait." He turned back to us. "Their cells have the ability to . . . they reconfigure themselves. They seem to understand where to go."

"Which means?" said Reese.

"They appear to communicate. Cell to cell. Normal organisms don't do that."

"Is that why they can heal things?" I asked.

"That's why they can heal things," said my dad.

"What about the sparkly thing, from Hadley Beach?" asked Reese.

"It has the same quality. The actual cell structure is different, but it acts the same. It has the same mutability."

"So Steve and Dave are from the ocean?" said Reese.

"They could be," said my dad. "Because of their abilities, they could probably exist anywhere. They could adjust to anything. They are, in a way, perfect beings."

Then I told my dad our news: that the boy who fell off the roof had lost his memory and Sheriff Moshofsky was going to arrest Dave and Steve.

"Are you serious?" said my father with new concern. "We can't let that happen."

"Yeah, but how do we find them?" I asked.

My father continued to wait for the person on the other line but began to dress at the same time. When the person finally came back, my dad told them he would call them in the morning.

"What are we going to do?" I asked.

"What else can we do?" said my father. "We're going to look for them."

34

The three of us got into my dad's Volvo. We bounced down the driveway to the road.

My dad began asking Reese and me everything we knew about Steve and Dave. Where had we first seen them? Where did they hang out? I told him everything I could think of, including the odd feeling that they had changed slightly when we told them they were so good-looking. They had become less good-looking. My father wondered why they would want to be so attractive in the first place.

"Probably because good-looking people get whatever they want," said Reese.

"Be serious," I said to Reese.

"No," said my father. "She might be right. Someone

observing human society from afar would think that was a good strategy."

Reese told him how they had reacted to the pizza, how they had spoken clumsily at first and gradually became fluent and eventually seemed to know every language.

"Fascinating," said my father. "It could be they weren't having trouble with the language; they were having trouble learning how to form the words with their mouths."

We began our search along the beach road. We drove slowly. We watched the beach. At one point we saw two people walking and we pulled over. Reese and I yelled to them, but it was just an old married couple out for a stroll.

We continued driving. We drove by the Delancy house, which was locked up because of the fire.

We drove through the woods. At one point I made my dad pull off to the side of the road. He turned off the car and the lights and we stood in the darkness. I don't know what I was thinking. I just had this idea that we needed to listen. Like if we could really *listen,* they would somehow communicate with us. I started apologizing about it, like probably it was a dumb idea, but Reese said no, she felt the same thing. My dad, of course, found all of this significant and asked us about it. We told him when we were lost in the woods, Steve and Dave seemed to listen to the birds and somehow figured out which way to go.

It wasn't working for us, though. We got back in the car and kept driving.

* * *

We cruised hotel row. We turned and drove on the back road that went behind the hotels. That was when I thought we were being watched. Reese thought so, too. We both turned at the exact same moment. A white sedan, far behind us, turned into a hotel parking lot. Besides that, there was nothing.

As we continued to drive, my dad told us more about the tests they had done on Steve's and Dave's cells. He explained that normal human cells, if you put them in a petri dish, just sat there. They might move around or expend energy in some way, but it was random. There was no coordination. But the cells of Steve and Dave seemed to understand one another. They moved around one another in patterns, as if they knew where they were going. My dad said it was like people at a party. Normal human cells act like people who don't know each other. If someone doesn't introduce them, they don't talk or interact and the party never gets going. But the Steve and Dave cells were interacting from the moment they were put together. They were sharing information. Not only was it a better party, but they could do almost anything, because they could work together.

Finally, we gave up our search. We drove back along the beach toward our house. We drove slowly, like we did before. Reese and I had our windows open. For some reason we were still obsessed with the idea we might hear something. We were in a moving car, though, so all we heard was the wind.

Then we did hear something: a siren. Police lights began to flash behind us. It was Sheriff Moshofsky. He had come up behind us. Reese and I gripped each other's arms. He was motioning for us to pull over.

My dad steered the Volvo onto the shoulder and stopped. Reese and I watched while the sheriff came to the window.

"Hello, Sheriff," said my dad.

"Hello, Professor," said the sheriff.

The sheriff didn't say anything else. He just stood there.

"Can I help you with something?" asked my dad.

"No, sir," said the sheriff.

"Well, why are you stopping us?"

"It's not up to me, Professor," said the sheriff.

"What's not up to you?" said my dad.

"Nothing personal, you understand."

"No, I don't understand," said my father.

Suddenly another car pulled up, a plain white sedan. It stopped abruptly beside us. Four men got out. Then another white car came up behind that one. A third pulled in front of our car. Men came out of all three white cars. There were maybe ten men all together. Some had walkie-talkies; others, cell phones. They opened my father's door and pulled him out of the Volvo. My father demanded they identify themselves. One of the men addressed him as Professor Dalton. They were very respectful, but they were definitely taking him somewhere and they weren't messing around.

I got out and tried to fight through them to my dad. Two men grabbed me and pulled me back.

"Emily!" said my father as they forced him into the sedan. "It's all right. Go to Reese's. Stay there!"

Reese and I stood in shock as the car with my dad sped off. The other men began searching our Volvo. A tow truck appeared. They were going to tow the Volvo away. It was unbelievable.

"Sheriff Moshofsky, where are they taking him!" I demanded.

"They just want to ask him some questions."

"Well, why didn't they just ask him?" I said.

We watched while one of the men yanked everything out of my dad's glove compartment.

"Come on," said the sheriff. "I'll give you girls a ride home."

"We don't want a ride home!" I said. "I want to know where my father is going!"

"He'll be fine. They just want to talk to him."

A pickup truck had come down the road from the other direction. The driver slowed to look at the police car and the other cars stopped at odd angles in the middle of the road.

The passenger window of the pickup was open. It was Harold and Carl.

"Harold!" yelled Reese.

"Carl!" I yelled.

The pickup truck stopped. Reese and I ran to it. "Can you give us a ride home?" I said.

"I guess . . . ," said Harold. "What's up? What's the sheriff want?"

I turned back to Sheriff Moshofsky. "Harold's going to give us a ride home."

"Suit yourself," said the sheriff.

Reese and I scrambled into the pickup truck. A couple

of the men watched us. They weren't sure if they should let us go. Reese motioned for Harold to hit the gas. He did. As we sped away, Reese flipped them off through the back window.

"Jesus, don't do that," Harold told Reese. "Don't you know who that is? That's the FBI."

"Like I care!" said Reese.

"They've been in South Point all night, harassing people, asking questions," said Carl.

"They'd better not hurt my dad," I said numbly. "I don't care who they are."

35

Harold and Carl fell silent once we were away from the police cars. They knew how to joke around and make fun of people, but in a serious situation they weren't so sure of themselves.

I, of course, could only think of my father. "We have to follow those cars," I whispered to Reese. "To find out where my dad is."

"Harold," said Reese in her most commanding voice. "Turn around."

"What for?"

"I want you to follow those cars."

"How come?"

"Can you not argue and just do it please?" commanded Reese.

"They'll see us," said Carl.

"We can't lose them," I said softly. "They have my dad."

"You heard her," Reese told Harold. "We can't lose them."

Harold, who had never done us a favor or anything nice for us in all the years we'd known him, suddenly swung his truck in a wide circle and turned around. He drove back cautiously. When we came to the place where Sheriff Moshofsky had stopped us, the only cars left were my dad's Volvo and the tow truck hauling it away.

"Great," I said. "We've already lost them."

"Go faster," commanded Reese.

Harold did. The pickup had a lot of power and soon we were going eighty. The four of us, all crammed into the front seat together, stared forward at the road ahead. I gripped the dashboard. When we saw the brake lights of two of the white sedans far ahead of us, Harold slowed down. He kept his distance, but he kept them in sight. He seemed to know how to stalk another car. He probably followed tourist girls around like this.

After a couple miles the white sedans slowed and turned right onto a gravel road.

Harold, who had been silent for the last couple minutes, turned to Reese. "Now what?"

Reese looked at me. I stared ahead at the cars as they disappeared into the woods. "I don't know," I said.

"We can follow them," said Harold.

"But won't they see us?" said Reese.

"I know that road," said Carl. "That's the back way to Hadley Beach."

"Hadley Beach is where they found the blob," I reminded Reese.

Harold slowed as we approached the turn-off. There was still dust in the air where the sedans had driven.

Without prompting, Harold turned and continued the pursuit. He drove slowly, with only his parking lights on. The rest of us peered forward in the darkness, whispering warnings when he got too close to the edge.

We drove for several minutes like this. As we came over a slight hill, we spotted below us what looked like a construction site. There were five or six trailers in a row with several cars parked around them. All the cars were sedans. There were lights on in the trailers and a fence around them. But we were still too far away to really see anything.

Then a set of headlights turned on right in front of us. It was another white sedan; it had been parked out of sight on the side of the road. Now it pulled forward, blocking our way.

Harold stopped. The four of us watched while two men got out and came toward us. Reese, thinking fast, grabbed Carl and made him trade places, so we were boy-girl-boy-girl.

"You guys are our boyfriends," she whispered in the dark. "Pretend we're looking for a place to make out."

The two men approached the truck, one on each side. The one at Harold's window did the talking. "Can I help you?" he said.

"Uh, we're just cruising around," said Harold. "Lookin' for a place with the best view. If you know what I'm sayin'."

The man ignored Harold and shone his flashlight into the car. He checked all four of us. We looked like four teenagers in search of a make-out spot. Reese was a genius.

"Well, you can't cruise around here," said the man. "This is a restricted area."

"Yeah?" said Harold. "It didn't used to be. What's going on?"

The man stepped back. "If you'll turn your vehicle around and leave the area."

"Yeah, but what are you doing?"

"If you'll turn your vehicle . . . ," said the man.

That's when I saw Steve coming up behind him. He had a big stick. In perfect silence he pulled the stick back and swung it like a baseball bat and hit the man in the back of the head. The man slammed up against Harold's door and slid to the ground. Then the same thing happened at my window. The second guy's head suddenly thudded against the side of the pickup. He, too, crumpled to the ground. I just about jumped over Carl, I was so frightened. Then I saw Dave holding a cinder block. He was watching the man he had just flattened with a look of wonder and amazement.

As soon as the two men were down, Steve and Dave began dragging them off the road. One of them was completely unconscious.

"Whoa, holy Jesus, you killed that guy!" said Harold.

"Get out and help them!" yelled Reese. She pushed Harold out the door, who reluctantly grabbed a foot of the unconscious man. Harold and Steve dragged him into the woods.

Carl and I opened the door on our side. Dave was still staring at his victim. "You can heal them, right?" was the first thing I said.

Dave nodded that he could. He and I and Carl gripped the man's arm and dragged him to where the other guy was. When they were both together, Dave knelt over the two of them. Steve, meanwhile, ran to the car they had been sitting in. He sat in the driver's seat and began rummaging through the papers and looking at the computer that was set up in the dashboard. Reese and I ran to help.

Steve found something, stared at it, frowned, and handed it to Reese. "Read this," he said.

Reese and I looked at each other. Could he not know how to read? He could speak every language, but he couldn't read? Was that possible?

"You," he said. "You read this. Out loud!" He handed me a document. I started reading it. But I stopped because I was interrupting Reese.

"No, all at the same time," said Steve. He gave a paper to Carl and told him to read it. The three of us stood in the dark around the car, quietly reading as fast as we could.

Reese was the one who found it. The second document she read kept referring to "the New Branford Research Facility." That was a place where they did marine and animal research. My dad used to teach a summer class there.

"That must be it," I blurted. "That must be where they have the blob."

Dave and Harold, meanwhile, were still in the woods crouched over the two injured men. They had barely been there two minutes and one of the men was already groaning and waking up.

"We must go!" Steve said, getting out of the car.

Harold and Dave hurried toward the pickup.

"But what about my dad?" I said.

"Your dad is safe," said Steve. "This is the best place for him."

"How do you know?"

"We have been here for two days. All the scientists are here. He is no doubt learning a great deal."

"Are those guys okay?" said Reese, looking back at the two injured men, one of whom was trying to roll over.

Dave looked back at the two men. "They will feel nothing for many hours."

"Come," said Steve. "We must leave now!"

"Whoa, dudes, you should have seen that," Harold said as he climbed into his truck. "He brought that guy back to life! He was all glowin' and stuff."

Everyone got back in the pickup. Carl and Dave jumped in the back. Reese, Steve, and Harold and I all squeezed in the front.

Harold had just started the engine when we saw a car coming toward us from the trailer park. "Look!" said Reese.

"Uh-oh," said Carl from the back.

Harold showed a new determination. He expertly turned the pickup around and floored it. We flew down the dirt road in the other direction. We tore around bends, skidded through curves. We bounced wildly in the front seat; our heads banged on the roof. But it worked.

The car behind us never got close. We were out of the trees in three minutes. On the highway, Harold drove eighty again, away from town in case they tried to radio ahead.

"Will those two guys remember any of this?" Reese asked Steve.

"They won't remember anything that happened for the last week," he said.

"So we're off the hook, for now," I said.

"For now," said Reese. "But how long is that going to last?"

It was Reese's idea to go to her house. We drove there half-expecting the police or the FBI or someone else to be waiting for us. But no one was there, not even her parents. Harold pulled into the driveway and Reese led Steve and Dave down a trail to the lake that was behind their house. There was an old boathouse near the water, which Reese's parents shared with their neighbors. Reese unlocked the door and led Steve and Dave inside. Then Reese and I both ran back to the driveway where Harold and Carl were waiting for further instructions.

"Okay, you guys," Reese instructed them, "go back home and act like everything's normal. If anyone asks you, you just drove us home tonight."

Harold nodded, but he didn't move. "But like . . . ?"

"What, Harold?"

"If we're going to do all this, what are you going to do for us?"

"What do you want?"

"I dunno."

"Okay," said Reese. "How about I'll be your girlfriend for a week?"

"Really?" said Harold. "And make out and stuff?"

"No, just your girlfriend."

"But wait, if you're my girlfriend, wouldn't we make out?"

"All right, one make-out session. Maybe."

"And me and Emily, too?" said Carl.

"That's up to Emily," said Reese.

They all looked at me.

"Sure, whatever," I said. "Same as Reese. *Maybe.*"

"All right," said Harold, grinning. "But when?"

"When all of this is completely over."

"When will that be?"

"The sooner you get out of here, the sooner that will happen. Now go!"

36

Back inside the boathouse, Reese lit a candle and we tried to clean up and make things comfortable for Steve and Dave. There was a dusty old couch and some deck chairs to sit on. I found a broom and swept while Reese began putting newspaper over the tiny windows so we wouldn't be seen.

While we did that, Steve and Dave both collapsed on the old couch. Dave looked like he was unconscious. Steve still had some of the documents from the car. He studied them in the candlelight.

"Can you read?" I said.

"I am learning."

"But don't you know all languages?"

"We know the sound of them, not what they look like."

Reese finished covering the windows and knelt over Dave. He did not look good. Neither of them did. They had been hiding in the woods for two days. As my eyes adjusted, I could see that they both needed to shave. And they were both skinny, much skinnier than they'd been when we first met them. Steve's hands shook as he held the paper.

"What's wrong with you guys?" Reese murmured as she folded Dave's arms over his chest and put a blanket over him.

Without thinking, I gripped Steve's wrist. He was terribly thin and he was trembling. "My god, you guys are starving!" I said.

"We need to eat," admitted Steve.

"Why haven't you?" said Reese.

"We don't know how," said Steve.

"We'll get you something. And you need water. Have you been drinking water?"

Steve shook his head no.

"We'll be right back," said Reese.

We ran up the path to Reese's house and went into the kitchen. Reese quietly went through the drawers. "White bread is probably best," she whispered.

"Yeah, stuff that's really bland. Instant oatmeal."

"And what to drink?" said Reese.

"Water, I guess."

"Juice, too, because they probably need the vitamins."

Reese found a cardboard box in the pantry. She filled it with a little of everything, and we ran back to the boathouse.

Dave was shaking terribly. We woke him up. We gave him water first. He tried to drink it and began choking and gasping and spitting it out.

"You don't *breathe it,*" said Reese. "You *drink* it."

"It's a different pipe," I said, pointing to my neck. "It goes in a different way."

He tried again and spit it out again. But on the third try he suddenly got it. He drank. He stared forward, bewildered, as he felt the water going into his stomach. He drank more. He guzzled. He drank a whole bottle of Reese's parents' fancy Italian mineral water.

Steve tried it more slowly. Tiny sips. He choked and gasped, but he finally got it, too. We told him to drink juice; it was better than water. They needed the sugar and the nutrients. He drank a whole bottle of Orangina.

We made them peanut butter sandwiches. Dave ate his like an animal. He ate another, eating so fast he almost threw up.

Steve did throw up at one point. He had to run outside. But he kept eating. They were amazed at the sensation of satisfying hunger. They couldn't believe how good it felt.

Reese, meanwhile, was touching Dave a lot. I was touching Steve, too. Even if you weren't touching them, being close to them, even now when they were in such terrible shape, you got this incredible warm feeling. It felt so good. It made you so happy.

Steve noticed what we were doing. "You must not touch us so much; it is bad for you," he said to Reese, who had her arm around Dave as he ate his sandwich. She also had her thigh pressed against his thigh and her foot wrapped around his ankle.

"Oh, was I touching him? I didn't mean to," lied Reese.

"Doesn't that feel better?" I asked Steve when the feeding frenzy was over. Reese had gone back to the house to get clothes and blankets.

"Yes," said Steve. "But now my stomach is too heavy and I feel like sleep."

"That's okay. You can sleep. You could shave, too," I said, touching his face. I kept touching it until he moved my hand away. It was weird how much you wanted to touch them. That warm, tingly thing—it was addicting.

Reese came back. She gave them some of her dad's shirts and cutoffs and a comforter. She sat on a box and stared at them. I stared, too. Dave was awake but practically unconscious. He was spread on the couch. He burped. Steve was sitting up, he looked groggy, but he picked up one of the documents and continued with his reading.

Reese and I did nothing for a while. Reese finally spoke up.

"So you guys are going to New Branford," she said. "To find the blob thing from the beach?"

"Yes," said Steve.

"Why is that thing so important?"

"The thing is part of us."

"What do you mean, part of you?"

"Like if you, Reese, were taken somewhere," said Steve. "Emily would try to find you. And return you to safety."

"But that thing didn't look like you. It was like a garbage bag or something."

"And I think . . . ," I added cautiously, "I think it might have been dead."

"It was not dead," said Steve. "It cannot be."

"Why not?"

"We don't die," said Steve.

"You don't?" said Reese. "What do you do?"

"Nothing."

"You live forever?"

"Yes."

"How can you do that?" said Reese.

"It is our nature."

"Huh," said Reese.

"Where do you live?" I asked.

"On the ocean floor," he said, shuffling through the papers.

I nodded. Reese said nothing. Steve studied his paper.

Reese found her voice. "That can't be right, though. How can you live in the ocean? Unless you're in a submarine or something. That's impossible."

"Reese," I said under my breath, thinking it was rude to accuse Steve of lying.

"What?" she said to me. "I'm serious. How could they?"

Steve looked up from his paper. "It is not impossible. Many things live there. Many species."

"My dad knew that," I blurted. "He knew you came from underwater. He figured out about your cells and how they can change."

"Is that true?" Reese asked him.

"It is not easy to change," said Steve. "We are human now. If we went in the ocean we would drown."

"But you can change back?" I asked.

"Yes, when the time comes. But that will also be very difficult."

Reese and I stared at them.

"Have you always lived on the bottom of the ocean?" I asked quietly.

"Yes."

"For how long?"

"For millions of years. To use your measurement system."

"Since the beginning of the planet?"

"Yes, roughly."

"Were you somewhere else before that?"

"Yes, we have been many places."

"Where are you from originally?" I said.

"I do not know."

"So you lived somewhere besides Earth?" asked Reese.

"We have lived on many planets. The planets change and we move from one to the other."

"Do you always live in the ocean of the planet?"

"Different planets have different kinds of oceans. The oxygen we breathe now, the 'air,' as you call it, is a kind of ocean. But the water is better. At the bottom levels there is safety."

"And you live forever?" said Reese.

"By your concept of time, yes. It is a different life cycle. We don't reproduce. We don't consume or create waste."

"What do you do then?" asked Reese.

"We have no activities. As you would understand them."

"But you must *do* something," said Reese.

Steve was reading and talking to us at the same time. "We listen."

"To what?"

"To everything," said Steve.

"Like to what, though?" I asked.

"The creatures of the sea. The microorganisms. And also the creatures in the lower atmosphere. All sound vibrations move through the water eventually. We hear everything. We hear the birds. The insects. Human speech."

"Can you understand it?"

"Of course. We have been listening to it since the birth of your planet."

"Wait," said Reese. "So you've been sitting at the bottom of the ocean, doing nothing but listening to us? For basically all of time? Are you like God? Or like friends of God or something?"

"No. We are an organism. Like you."

I glanced over at Dave. "Do you talk to one another?" I asked.

"No."

"Why not?"

"There is no need. We are not separate from one another."

"Don't you get bored?" said Reese.

"No."

"How long will you stay here?" I asked. "On Earth, I mean."

"Until your planet becomes uninhabitable."

"When will that happen?"

"It has begun. That is why the organism came to the surface. Your oceans are changing very quickly now. There are new toxins. Soon the Earth will be unable to sustain life. And then we will go. But the organism must be rescued first."

Reese and I stared at him. "Our oceans are becoming toxic?"

"Of course," said Steve. "You know that."

"We do?"

"Yes."

"How soon before the Earth can't sustain life?" I asked.

"In your time perspective, maybe some time from now. To our perspective, very soon."

Reese and I looked at each other.

37

Steve made us leave the boathouse after that. He and Dave needed to sleep. Reese and I went back to her house and slept in her bed.

The dreams that night were incredible, the best yet. At one point, I woke up and Reese was wrapped around her pillow with the biggest, happiest smile on her face. Another time I woke up and our backs were touching and we were both humming softly to ourselves, but in harmony, like the vibrations of our bodies were synchronized, even though we were fast asleep.

The next morning we jumped out of bed and sprinted to the boathouse. This time, Steve was fast asleep and it was Dave who was awake. He was trying to figure out how to eat the box of Cheerios we had brought him. He was studying the box. He had put a Cheerio in his mouth and was tentatively chewing it, unsure if it was food.

Reese assured him it was and proved it by grabbing a fistful of Cheerios and mashing them into her mouth. The crumbs poured down her front and we both laughed. Dave did, too, though the act of laughing was strange for him, you could tell. It was so funny watching an alien learning how to be a human. Also, he was not in pain anymore. Not at all. Could he have been suffering from hunger the whole time?

After Reese stopped making a pig of herself, Dave and Reese and I went to the lake. Reese and I crouched on the little boat dock and rinsed our faces with the lake water (we had forgotten to take showers, we were in such a hurry to get near Dave and Steve). Dave stayed closer to the trees, out of sight, but when it seemed safe, he came onto the dock. He leaned down, cupped his hands in the water, and put the water on his face. He grinned at the sensation and did it again.

A fish jumped on the lake somewhere. Reese sat down next to Dave. "So is it true what Steve said, you guys can hear fish talk?"

"It is not speech, as you think of it, but there are vibrations."

"Wow," I said. I sat down, too.

"What do fish say?" asked Reese.

Dave was washing his arms. "The same as every other creature."

"What's that?"

"They say, *I am here; where are you?*"

"What do birds say?" I said.

"The same, *I am here; where are you?"*

"So everyone just says that?" said Reese.

Dave nodded. "That is the basic message of all creatures. Even the ants in the ground. Even the viruses in your body."

"I have a virus in my body?" exclaimed Reese.

"All humans do," said Dave. "Many of them. And bacteria. And other microscopic beings you don't yet know about. You are a kind of hotel. And all the things that live in you communicate."

"You can hear a *virus*?" I asked. "What does a virus say?"

"The same. *I am here; where are you?"*

"But not everyone just says *that,"* said Reese. "Because humans, we can say all sorts of things. Because we have language."

"All creatures have language," said Dave. "Humans say the same thing. All the creatures say the same thing."

"But humans talk about other things," argued Reese. "We talk about the weather and about clothes and TV shows."

"Yes, but the basic message is the same."

Reese didn't agree. "But if I say to Emily, *I like your shirt; where did you get that?* I'm not saying, *I am here; where are you?"*

Dave was still staring into the water. "All communication serves the same purpose: to create a whole out of individuals. With every word you speak, every message you send out, with your clothes or your gestures, or the expression on your face, you repeat the same message:

This is who I am; who are you? You do this to define the group, so that everyone will know their place. So everyone will know their purpose."

"But what if you're just talking about a movie?" said Reese.

"You think you are talking about a movie. But you are only using the movie to define yourself. You are always indicating what your place in the group is. You constantly say to the others: *I am this way; what way are you?* You do this because you need the group. And the more communication there is, the more efficient the group becomes."

"Wow," I said.

Some birds were cawing in the trees above us. "Birds are great communicators," said Dave. "Better than humans."

"They can't be *better* than humans," said Reese.

"Yes, much better. That is why they have been here so long," said Dave. "They were here before you."

"No way," said Reese. "Birds were not here before humans."

"They were here when the dinosaurs died," said Dave thoughtfully. He squinted up at a group of crows sitting on a treetop. "They saw it. They speak of it. They remember it."

Later, Steve woke up. He wanted to eat more. He said he could feel the food being converted to energy in his body. He kept looking at his arms and his legs. He thought it was fascinating.

"You should hang out with my dad," I told him. "He

loves talking about stuff like food being converted to energy."

"Your father is a very intelligent man," said Steve. "He is very unusual."

I totally turned red when he said that, I was so proud. It was so fun to hang out with Steve and Dave. They made you so unbelievably happy.

But Steve didn't want to hang out. He thought Reese and I should go to the beach. He thought we should let the sheriff and everyone else see that we were living our normal lives. That would give Steve and Dave another day of eating and resting. They needed to regain their strength if they were going to find the blob.

Reese agreed to go to the beach, but only if they swore they wouldn't leave and they would let us help with whatever they did.

They agreed. Though I don't know if aliens who live at the bottom of the ocean can really swear to things. But we did what they told us; we walked back to Reese's house and got our beach stuff.

That's when my dad called. Reese answered and gave me the phone. I was so relieved to hear his voice. He didn't have much time to talk. He said in a slow, careful voice that the authorities were very preoccupied with gathering information regarding the organism from Hadley Beach. I suspected this meant they were listening in and not to say anything about Steve and Dave. So I didn't. My dad said he would be home soon. They weren't holding him in a legal way; it was more an unofficial quarantine of all the people who had contact with the organism. It was actually good because he was with other scientists and they were getting a chance to compare notes. He told me not to worry; he was safe. He wasn't sure when he would be home, probably in the next day or two. I said okay. I told him I loved him and hung up.

Then Reese and I went to the beach.

38

Walking to town, I began to understand why Steve had warned us not to touch them too much. That warm feeling you got when you touched them, it was staying in me now. It was affecting my senses. I was seeing things differently. Colors looked different and everything had a strange, slightly transparent quality I had never noticed before. It was a little unnerving; it was like some part of Steve's and Dave's experience of things had transferred into me.

We arrived at Antonio's Pizza Palace. Reese wasn't saying much. We got specials and sat outside at one of the tables. That's when things really got weird. I looked into the street and objects began to shimmer and change and I felt a strange liquid sensation in my stomach, like the ocean was pulling me or the sky was reflecting through me. Reese was having the same thing. She didn't say anything, but I knew it was happening to her, too. In some way, I could almost feel her emotions and thoughts. It kind of creeped me out. Then, as I tried to eat my pizza, I watched the people at the next table talking and I thought I could see the sound waves actually moving through the air. It was like everything was made of vibrations and electrical fields and everything moved and flowed and changed—even the greasy tabletop was suddenly transparent and made of nothing. I touched the napkin dispenser, to test that it was real. I touched my arm; I touched the pizza crust from the slice I had finished.

Reese put down her pizza. "I can't . . . eat this," she said quietly.

"I know."

"Do you feel like *really* weird?" she asked.

I nodded that I did. "It's like the dreams. But now it's the middle of the day."

She stared at her pizza for a second. Then she lowered her head into her hands. Tears came to her eyes. I understood. I felt like crying, too. All this weirdness, it was very stressful. I gave her my napkin and put my hand on her back. But even that did something. It wasn't like touching Steve or Dave, but there was definitely a tiny flow of something when my hand was on her back. It felt like I joined with her, like we came together and understood each other in some way, like we both knew things, things humans weren't even supposed to know. I took my hand away.

Reese collected herself. She sat up and dabbed her eyes. "I don't think I can handle this," she said.

"Maybe we should be more careful," I said. "And not be around them so much."

"But we have to! We have to help them. They don't know certain things."

"I know. But what if they're brainwashing us in some way? What if they're making us help them?"

"No, they're not," cried Reese. "They just want to get their friend and go back to the ocean."

"Maybe. But who knows?"

"Oh my god, if we don't hang out with them tonight I'm going to have a nervous breakdown," said Reese.

"We have to be strong," I told her. "If not for us, for them."

We went to the beach. We found Justin and Nick and Sheila. They were very glad to see us. They gathered around us as we put our towels down.

"Is Luke around?" asked Reese as she straightened her towel in the sand.

"He's up in the parking lot," said Sheila. "Watching everyone with binoculars."

"Figures," I said.

"Don't gather around us," said Reese. "Everyone act normal."

They obeyed; everyone spread out on their towels and tried to look bored like they normally did. But everyone wanted to hear what had happened. They kept bugging us. Reese wouldn't say. I told Sheila and Nick about my father and about the FBI taking him away with the other scientists. Sheila said the FBI had been interviewing people at the hotel. Apparently it led to a big scene, with the families at the hotel complaining about the prowler and everyone getting really paranoid and accusing one another and yelling at the hotel manager. Finally the hotel manager made the FBI leave, since they didn't have a warrant and they were causing so much trouble.

Later I went for a walk with Nick. We didn't talk too much, but he held my hand, which was such a nice thing to do. But I was feeling like Reese. All I could think about was Steve and Dave. They had totally taken over every thought I had.

But Nick was so cool. He didn't complain or say anything. And when we sat on this log up the beach he put his hand on my shoulder and rubbed my neck and said how weird a summer it was. I smiled at him and we kissed a little. It was nice.

39

"Steve? *Dave!*" shrieked Reese that night, when we returned from the beach. It was dark inside the boathouse. She banged on the door. We were both terrified they had left.

They hadn't. The door opened and Dave let us in. They had eaten every bit of food we had left for them.

"We need more food," said Steve.

"Jeez," said Reese. "You ate all that?"

"We need more," said Steve.

"Aren't you full?" said Reese.

"What's full?" said Dave.

"When your stomach's full?" said Reese, touching her stomach. "When you can't eat any more?"

They both looked down at their stomachs. "How do you know when it's full?" said Dave.

But Reese was not going to be distracted. She had been in a very bad mood all day and it was because of Steve and Dave and now they were going to hear about it.

She made them sit on the couch. She stood over them. "I have a question for you two, and I want it answered, *now.*"

"Yes?" said Steve. He looked much better now. So did Dave. They were both back to being nearly Brad Pitt–like. They were handsome and their skin glowed with health.

"If you can't die, why are you so worried about your friend?" she said.

Steve and Dave looked at each other. "Because we cannot leave him," said Dave.

"But why can't you, if he can't die? Why don't you just wait until the science people get bored with him and dump him back in the ocean?"

"They won't do that," said Steve. "They will discover his healing qualities. They will try to find the rest of us. They will do terrible things."

"Like what?"

"Like try to kill us or capture us, or reproduce us in some way."

"Oh," said Reese. She hadn't thought of that.

"We would be very valuable to your race," said Dave.

"So valuable," said Steve, "that your species would do anything to have us. You would kill each other. You would destroy your entire world."

"Well, according to you," said Reese, getting mad again, "we're destroying our entire world anyway."

"Yes," said Steve. "That is true."

"And even if you get him, or her, or whatever it is," continued Reese. "Then what will you do? Go back and sit on the bottom of the ocean some more?"

"Yes," said Steve.

"And what happens to us?" said Reese, pointing at me and her.

"You will remain here, as you were."

"We will remain here *to die,* you mean."

"Humans don't really die," explained Steve. "They are . . . recycled."

"You are all one organism," said Dave. "The concept of individuality is an illusion."

"In other words," Reese said, "I'm right. You *are* going to leave us here to die."

"That is your way," said Steve. "You are born and you live and you die. It is your nature. You are fulfilling your role."

"But what if I don't want to fulfill my role?" said Reese. She started to cry again. I went to her, but she pushed me away. She went to Dave instead. He put his arms around her and she clung to him.

"No, you cannot have too much contact," said Steve. "You must not. It is bad for you. It is bad for us. Release her."

Dave tried to get Reese off him. But she wouldn't let go. I finally had to pull her away.

40

That night, Reese's parents came home. The Ridgleys never went to the lake, so Steve and Dave were safe in the boathouse. But Reese and I had to act normal around her parents. We had to have dinner with them. It was pretty easy for me, because I was always polite around the Ridgleys. Reese, though, was irritable and impatient and she could barely get through dinner.

Somehow we managed. Afterward, we told her parents we had to meet some people on the beach. We walked straight to the General Store to buy more food for Dave and Steve. We got high-protein stuff: tuna fish, peanut butter, cottage cheese. As we came out of the store, we saw Harold and Carl hanging out in their pickup truck. I thought they were going to do something horrible, like make us be their "girlfriends," but they wanted to help and offered to drive us back to Reese's.

They dropped us off and we snuck around Reese's house and went to the boathouse. Inside, Dave and Steve had found some old paperbacks and were reading them in the faint candlelight. Dave was reading a ragged, coverless copy of *Codependent No More* and Steve was reading *Star Trek #17: The High Priestess Returns.*

"Are you understanding it?" asked Reese.

Steve nodded. "The story of *Star Trek* is based on the idea that every place in the universe would benefit from a visit by your species."

"It's just a TV show," said Reese.

"You are our *enablers,*" said Dave, looking up from his book. "You bring us what we want and we give you nothing in return."

"That's right," joked Reese. "You give us precious little, I would say."

"What food have you brought?" said Steve.

Reese began to unpack the bags. Steve picked up a can of tuna. Dave began to eat peanut butter out of the jar with his fingers.

"No!" said Reese, pulling Dave's hand out of the jar. "You eat that with bread. Or off a spoon." Then she turned to Steve, who was studying the tuna can. "You oughta recognize that. That's a fish. Like where you come from."

That night my dad called. Reese and I were in her room, getting ready for bed. Reese's mom answered, and I took the call downstairs. My dad said the same thing as before and, like before, never really gave me a chance to talk, probably so I wouldn't reveal anything. He said all the scientists would be going home soon. He also said some very important people from Washington were involved now.

In bed, I told Reese what my dad had said.

"Would the government try to kill Steve and Dave?" she asked me.

"Why would they?"

"Maybe they couldn't. Since they don't die."

"But maybe they could," I said. "Since they're in human form."

"We should have asked them that."

"There's all these things I want to ask them, but I never remember when I'm around them."

"I think I'm in love with them," said Reese.

"With *them*?" I said. "With Steve, you mean? Or Dave?"

"With both of them. I don't ever want to be away from them."

"I know what you mean," I said. "Don't our lives seem pointless when they're around?"

"Pointless and short."

"But that's not true, though, right?" I said. "Because we have our role, and we do it as best we can."

"Yeah, but what's our role?"

"You know, we love each other and help each other or whatever. Our fellow humans."

"Yeah, I guess. The way they describe it, we're no better than ants. Or germs."

I shifted in the bed, turning away from Reese. "Isn't it cool, though, that all they do is listen?" I whispered.

"They could do anything and be anything, but instead they sit silently on the bottom of the ocean, listening to things."

"Think how noisy that would get. If you could hear every sound on the planet."

"But think of the knowledge you would have," I said. "You would know everything. You would have heard every professor, every leader, every scientist. They probably heard Socrates and people like that."

"They've heard people having sex. They've probably heard *me* having sex," said Reese.

"Maybe they don't know what sex is."

"I don't even care. I just hope I have the dreams tonight." Reese sighed.

"We will; of course we will. We spent all night with them."

"I can't wait."

"Me, neither."

"Good night, Emily."

"Good night, Reese."

Part FOUR

41

The dreams came over me differently that night. First I dreamed I was with my dad and we were talking to Steve and Dave. They told us how little time we had. They said there were places in northern Canada where people would survive for a few more decades. The rest of the human race would die very quickly. This would all happen very soon. Within years maybe, or within months.

When I woke up I didn't know if this was real or a dream. I also wondered if Steve and Dave had put this dream in my brain to help my father and me survive. They always tried to help people when they could. At the same time, didn't they say that the human race was just one big organism? What was the point of trying to save my dad and me? It was all very creepy. I finally fell back asleep and then I had the usual dreams, big waves of happiness and joy and flying through the sky and the sun warming everything and filling my senses . . . but then I woke up again.

I turned to Reese. I didn't see her in the dark, so I reached my hand out. There was a tangle of blankets but no Reese. I reached more. My stomach filled with dread. She was not there. She was not in the bed.

I sat up. I looked around the room. No Reese. I got up as quietly as I could. I put on my shorts and my tennis shoes. I crept to the door and looked into the hall. I quietly moved down the stairs and out the back door. I thought, *What if Steve and Dave left and took her?* A shudder went through me. I hurried across the back porch, down the steps, down the wet, grassy path to the boathouse. The sky was that eerie gray just before the dawn. The woods were silent except for the occasional chirp of a bird.

I got to the boathouse and snuck forward. It looked the same as last night.

I opened the door. The first thing I saw was Steve, on the floor. We had given him two sleeping bags to put on the floor. He lay there, on his side, fast asleep. Dave was on the couch, as we had left him, buried under several blankets. Then I saw the hand. There was a pale hand sticking out from under Dave's blankets. I stepped over Steve, gripped the blankets, and yanked them back. It was Reese. In her underwear. She was wrapped around Dave, who was fast asleep, as dead asleep as Steve was. Reese was twitching slightly. Her eyelids were fluttering like she was having nightmares.

I grabbed her arm. "Reese! Reese! What are you doing?"

Her eyes opened, but she was completely passed out. Then her eyes rolled back in her head.

This was not good. I grabbed her harder and pulled. Dave fell off the couch. He was in boxers and a T-shirt, clothes Reese had given him. He woke up. Steve woke up. I pulled Reese upright, but she was still not quite conscious.

"What is she doing?" said Steve.

"She was sleeping with Dave," I said. "She was under the covers with him."

"Oh no," said Steve. "That is very bad." He got up. He went to her, gripped her face, studied her eyes. "You cannot have prolonged contact with us!"

This put me in a panic. "She'll be okay, though?" I said. "When she wakes up?"

He continued to study her face. "Why was she here? I told you both not to do this!"

"It's not my fault. She snuck out here by herself. She couldn't help it. She wants the dreams."

"Why can't your species control itself!" said Steve angrily.

Dave and Steve laid her back on the couch. She was trembling now. And shaking.

"I have to call an ambulance," I said as I wrapped a blanket around her. "We have to do something."

"There is nothing to do," said Steve. "An ambulance will not help."

"Can *you* do something? Can you heal her?"

"She has already been healed. That's what contact does. Everything is brought into harmony by contact.

But the human organism can't accept harmony. Her body reacts like this because it does not understand. She must now revert to her natural state."

"She won't die, though?"

"On the contrary, she is experiencing life everlasting. For the moment," said Steve, watching her. "She is further from death at this moment than any human will ever be."

"Oh my god, Reese," I said, trying to hug her. But when I touched her I got a jolt of that warm current. She was as full of the strange energy now as Steve and Dave. Maybe more.

"It is perhaps a good time for us to go," said Steve.

"No!" I said. "You can't leave! You said we could go with you. We want to help you."

"Reese cannot help us now."

"But I can. And my father. My father wants to see you again. He needs to talk to you. He's protected you. He's protected you all along."

Steve looked at me. He looked at Reese. "All right. If you wish. *But you must not have contact.* Our powers are not unlimited in this state. We must conserve our energy."

"What does that mean?" I asked.

"It means we lose a little every time you touch us."

Reese groaned and rolled sideways. They had lost a lot on her.

"If you want to help us," said Steve, "you will have to control yourself. Can you do that?"

I swallowed. "I can't speak for anyone else. But I can. I think. . . ."

"All right then," said Steve, who had trouble staying mad. "The first thing . . . I suppose . . . we will need a car."

Getting a car became my job. I figured my best chance was Harold and his pickup truck. In the predawn gray, I started walking toward his house.

No cars were on the road. There were no signs of people. Other stuff was going on, though. A group of birds above me was squawking and shifting positions in the trees. I squinted up at them as I walked. The birds were warning one another and arguing. There was a territorial dispute. The problem was: a new batch of birds had appeared in one of the big trees and the birds who normally hung out there were not happy about it. They were spreading the alarm. Meanwhile, their leader was addressing the new birds directly. He was demanding they leave.

The new birds didn't want to; their reply was, *We*

heard this was where everyone was. The original group of birds was not accepting this. They already had their social order established and they didn't want to rearrange everything for the new birds. Especially the leader, who had fought many battles to get where he was.

Then all arguments stopped. A swarm of bugs had appeared on the pond to lay their eggs. The birds instantly forgot the dispute and they all flew toward the swarm to eat.

Now it was the bugs who sounded the alarm. They were like: *Oh no, here come the birds.* But they didn't try to get away. Since there were thousands of them and only a few dozen birds, they went about their business. The idea among the bugs seemed to be: *They can't eat us all. We will lay our eggs. . . .*

I walked a little ways before I realized what had just happened. I had *heard* those birds. Or had I? Was it possible? Or was I just making up in my head what I *thought* they were saying? And what about the bugs? They didn't make any noise at all. So what was I *hearing*?

Meanwhile, in front of me, a chipmunk scurried away from the road and deeper into the woods as I passed. He seemed to be upset by my presence; he didn't like the smell of humans. There was other roadside activity as well. Smaller birds were maneuvering in the lower brush. They, too, were arguing about territory. I tried to listen, but there was now so much going on, I wasn't sure what I was hearing. There were bugs, bees, spiders; even the leaves seemed to communicate. They were arranging themselves to catch the first rays of sunlight. They knew where the sun would be, which direction it would come from; they seemed to tell one another these things.

Then I saw a heron standing by the ditch up ahead of me. He was looking for tadpoles in the ditch water. He wasn't happy to see me and he watched me very closely. I felt a terrible sense of loneliness coming from him. He spent his whole life by himself. Some animals were like that. The males especially. The females at least had offspring to love and worry about.

I kept walking. A baby frog hopped onto the road. I reached down and picked him up and carried him a little way. He let me hold him. He sat in my hand looking up at me. I understood at that moment why Earth creatures "recycle," why they live and die and new creatures are constantly born. It was so there would always be young creatures on the planet. Because young creatures trust and are open and welcome the world. They balance out the bad parts of our nature with their gentleness.

43

I got to Harold's house. It was on the edge of town. It wasn't the nicest house. A rusty old car sat on blocks in the driveway. Some broken toys were scattered across the yard.

I went to the door. I opened the screen door and knocked. It was awfully early. Nothing happened and I knocked again. This time the door opened and a little girl stood before me. She didn't speak.

"Hi there," I said. "Are you Harold's sister? Is your brother awake?"

She looked at me with the biggest, most perfect eyes. She put her fingers in her mouth.

A large, knobby hand gripped her shoulder and

pulled her away from the door. It was Harold. He was half-asleep. "Oh. Emily. What are you doing?"

"Hi," I said. I motioned for him to step outside and shut the door. He did and I said, "Remember how Reese said she would be your girlfriend for a week?"

"Yeah?"

"How would you like her to be your girlfriend for two weeks?"

Harold frowned. "You don't have to offer me stuff. I know you need help."

We drove back to Reese's in Harold's pickup. On the way, I made Harold swing by my house. I needed to change my clothes and get some clean underwear. When we pulled up, the Volvo was in front. I ran up the stairs and my dad was there! He was lying on the couch with his blanket over him!

"Oh my god! Dad!" I said, running across the room and jumping on top of him.

"Emily! Oh my!" he said as he tried to avoid getting squished.

I got off him, but I kept hugging him. I couldn't let go.

"Honey, calm down," said my dad. "You have to tell me: Where are Steve and Dave?"

I told him. I told him everything. I told him Steve and Dave were aliens just like he said. And they lived underwater just like he said. I told him the white blob on the beach was their friend and they were going to rescue him. They were going to do it soon. Tonight maybe.

My dad nodded. But he didn't look happy.

"What's the matter?" I said.

"I don't know if they can."

"Of course they can," I said. "They can do anything. They learned to read in one day."

"The New Branford facility is on high security. There are armed guards. One of the scientists I talked to this morning was just there."

"But they're *aliens*. They can do anything."

"But they're in human form. They can only do what a human can do."

"But what about the dreams?"

"The dreams are nice," said my father. "But they don't stop bullets."

"Uh, hello?" came a voice from behind me. It was Harold, whom I had forgotten about. My dad didn't recognize him and immediately stood up. He winced with pain. He grabbed his hip.

"What is it?" I asked. "Is your hip hurting again?"

My dad shook his head. "It's all right. It's just stiffened up."

"But I thought it was healed?"

"Arthritis is a natural occurrence. It comes back," said my father. "Especially when you're old."

"Oh, *Dad*!" I said. I hugged him one more time.

The three of us got into Harold's pickup truck. We drove to Reese's. I told my dad about Reese. How she had fallen asleep next to Dave. And how she had gotten really sick.

"Of course," said my father, nodding. "The euphoria Steve and Dave produce could become addictive. How could it not be?"

We got out of the truck. We walked around the Ridgleys' house, but as we did, who appeared but Mrs. Ridgley. I had totally forgotten about her.

"Professor Dalton, so nice to see you," she said. She had her gardening hat on, and her gloves.

"Hello, Peggy," said my dad.

"If I'd known you were coming, I would have made lemonade," said Mrs. Ridgley. "It's getting warm again. After that strange cold spell."

"I would love some lemonade," said my father. "But actually, at the moment, the girls and I are taking a sample of the lake water. It's a little experiment we're conducting."

"Oh, how interesting," said Mrs. Ridgley, smiling coyly. "An *experiment.* I quite liked science when I was younger." Was she flirting with my dad? Old people were so weird.

"Yes, and I'm afraid we really need to get to it," said my dad. "You know how the girls are; they can't be denied anything."

"Where is Reese?" said her mother, looking absently around the yard. "She is around, isn't she? I think we grounded her."

"She's already down at the lake," I said. "She's waiting for us."

"Oh, I see. Well, tell her not to go anywhere. It's almost time for lunch."

44

My father, Harold, and I walked down the trail toward the boathouse. My father was limping again. He pulled the pipe out of his shirt pocket and bit it like he always does. It occurred to me that he did this because he was in pain. All these years he had been in pain, and he never said a word.

Then I felt something. It was in the bushes by the trail. It was a sense of alarm; a predator was present and the smaller birds were trying to get away, and the mice, too. I glanced into the woods and sure enough, Reese's cat was crouched in a clearing, waiting to pounce.

It was the same as when I heard the birds that morning. What if I kept hearing things? I couldn't listen to every bug and mouse and bird I encountered. I could barely deal with my fellow humans.

Meanwhile my dad was getting excited. He couldn't wait to ask Steve and Dave about every detail of their existence. He hurried to the door of the boathouse. I checked behind us to make sure Mrs. Ridgley wasn't following.

My dad bit his pipe and knocked lightly. Steve opened the door. He smiled at my father, but his first concern was food. Had we brought any? We hadn't. I forgot; I should have brought some from my house.

My dad saw Reese on the couch. She was covered with a blanket. He went to her and knelt down and checked her pulse. He stroked her hair and pulled her eyelids back. Steve and Dave knelt down, too. "She will be all right?" said Steve.

"I was going to ask you that," said my dad.

"I think so," said Steve. "Her body will return eventually to how it should be."

My dad put his hand on her back to check her breathing. But when he did his expression changed. He took his hand off her back and put it back on. He touched Steve. At first Steve tried to move his hand away, but my father motioned to let him do it; he was doing an experiment. He touched Steve and let go. He touched Reese and let go.

"Very interesting," he said.

"What is it?" I said.

"She is giving off the same low-voltage current as Steve."

"Maybe it's because she got so much of it last night," I said.

"Yes," said my dad. "That might be."

Harold spoke up. "Uh, you guys, I should probably move my pickup. . . ."

My dad had taken charge of things. He turned to Steve and Dave. "I assume you want to rescue the organism. If so, you're going to need a plan."

Steve nodded thoughtfully. "Yes, it is true."

"Why don't you just kill everyone, and heal them later?" offered Harold.

Steve shook his head. "We are losing our healing powers. We are losing all our abilities. That is why we need to act now."

"Well, I know the building," offered my father. "That'll help. And if we can get inside, I know where the lab is. It won't be easy."

Steve thought about it. He stared at Reese. He looked sorry he had made her sick. He looked unsure of what he should do.

It occurred to me that he was becoming more human every day; whatever his strange powers were, they were indeed spreading to the people around him. We were becoming more like him. He was becoming more like us. It was a form of communication. And it was happening whether he wanted it to or not.

45

It was decided to do nothing until nightfall. My dad would stay with Steve and Dave and make sure Reese was okay.

I was sent to the beach with Harold. As we drove I was still "hearing" things. Like sitting beside Harold, I was picking up moods or attitudes, and weird things about his personality. I guess it was chemicals or vibrations, or maybe pheromones. Whatever it was, there sure was a lot of it. One thing was clear: *humans are always communicating*. Talking was only one of the ways we did it, and in a way, it was the least revealing.

One thing I sensed from Harold was how happy he felt with all this stuff happening. He was a person who needed a mission, or a cause. Helping Steve and Dave had finally given him one. I could also see that despite being a jerk to the tourists, he was actually a very loyal person. He would die for you. He really would. He was like a soldier ant; he had a soldier mentality. That's why he seemed so pathetic hanging around South Point all these years. He had nothing to fight for. He never got to be who he really was.

I didn't mention this of course. I was "hearing" things all over the place and it was getting a little confusing. It happened when we stopped at the gas station. I was watching the Exxon guy pumping our gas and I suddenly knew all these things about him, too. And then, in the trash can by the squeegees, there were several hundred insect conversations going on at once. I couldn't understand much of that, except that they were all very excited and happy about whatever was in the garbage. It was something with lots of sugar. Insects really like sugar, but I guess I already knew that.

At the beach, Harold dropped me off. He had to work at the garage with Carl that afternoon. I went into the restrooms by the parking lot to change. When I came out, Luke pulled up in his police car. He and Jimmy were cruising the beach. Luke saw me and waved me over.

"Hey, Emily," he said.

"Hey, Luke," I answered.

"Where's Reese?"

"At her mom's. She got grounded."

"Your dad back?"

"Yeah, they let him go."

"Wonder what that was like?" Luke asked casually. "Being held by the Feds, by the FBI. . . ."

"It wasn't bad," I said. "They just wanted to keep everyone together. I guess that thing they found on the beach might have been toxic."

"Yeah," said Luke. "With all the crap they dump in the ocean nowadays. Probably everyone will get cancer. Then say good-bye to the tourist trade."

I nodded my agreement.

"Whatever happened to those exchange students?" said Luke.

"I don't know," I said. "I thought you were going to arrest them."

"Nah," he said. "They pulled us off that. The Feds are going after them now."

"Really?" I said as casually as I could. "When are they going to do that?"

"I dunno. Word went out this morning. They're probably on them right now. The Feds, they can find anyone. The trouble is, you never find out what happened."

I nodded.

"Who were those guys?" said Luke, suddenly lowering his voice. "I mean, who were they *really*?"

"I really don't know," I said.

"They were some pretty weird dudes."

I shrugged. "You know as much as I do."

"Some strange stuff going on around this town," said Luke, shaking his head. He was like Harold, I understood at that moment, another soldier with nothing to fight for. Were all boys like that?

* * *

After that I trudged down the beach. Nick and everyone else were on the far end. When I appeared they gathered around me.

"Don't talk to me," I said. "Act natural. The FBI is looking for Steve and Dave. They could be up in the parking lot."

"Jeez," said Nick. "This just gets worse and worse."

"But my dad is okay," I said. "That's the good news."

"Where's Reese?" whispered Sheila, acting like she was brushing the sand off her towel.

"She's . . . she's back at her house."

"What are they going to do? Steve and Dave, I mean?" asked Nick.

"I don't know. But they'll be leaving soon."

"They were so cool," said Nick. "I wish I could see them again."

"What was so cool about them?" said Justin. "They sound like geeks."

"I'm sorry I didn't get to meet them," said Sheila.

"They're incredible," I said quietly. "They change you. They change everything."

"I know," said Sheila. "I can see it on your face."

46

It was a difficult afternoon at the beach. For one thing I was afraid to be around Nick. I was afraid that something would pass between us, that I would "hear" something, or suddenly know something about him I wasn't supposed to. With all this other stuff going on, I wanted whatever happened with Nick and me to be natural, or at least natural in a human sense. Everything became so fantastic with Steve and Dave around. But Nick had been fantastic before that. I wanted to save that feeling for when everything was normal again.

It wasn't easy staying away from him. For one thing, after a couple hours on the beach I realized I hadn't eaten anything since the day before. I was so hungry my legs were shaking. Sheila and Nick took me to Antonio's and we all got specials.

Maybe that's why everything seemed so weird, because I was so hungry. I chomped down on my pizza, but it was too hot and it burned the roof of my mouth. Nick gave me water and told me to slow down. He wanted to know what the plan was. How were Steve and Dave going to get their friend? I told him the truth, that I didn't know, and that my dad thought it might be impossible.

"That's so cool they want to save their friend," said Nick.

It made me happy he said that. It was such a Nick thing to say.

After pizza, Nick and Sheila wanted to walk me back to my house. They wanted to help. They were angry at Luke and Sheriff Moshofsky and the FBI and all the other people who wouldn't leave Steve and Dave alone. But I could also see they were kind of . . . *influenced.* Like I remembered when Reese and I first met Steve and Dave, we wanted to help them, too. Like before we even knew what their problem was. Their need for help seemed to *influence* everyone who came into contact with them.

Sheila had a cell phone, so I took her number and told her I would call her if we needed anything. I started walking back to my house. Nick wanted to walk with me part of the way.

"Listen," he said. "Whatever they do, I want to be part of it."

"Maybe you shouldn't, though," I told him. "It's getting so scary, and dangerous."

"But I want to help. And you're going. It's not safe for you, either. At least I'm a boy."

"What does that mean?"

"I'm good at that stuff. Sneaking around. Stealing stuff. Running from the cops."

"I'm sure you are," I said. I was walking quickly now. I looked down at my feet. "It's just that . . . I don't want to be around you too much."

"Why not?"

"Something's happened to me. I . . . I can hear things now."

"What things?"

"It's from being around Steve and Dave. I can hear animals and birds communicating. Anything that's alive. Frogs even. Bugs."

"You mean you can hear them talk?"

"I don't understand everything they're saying. I just get the sense of it. That's why Steve and Dave know so much. They don't have the boundaries we have. They communicate with everything. On every level."

"Well, what's wrong with that? That's good. Maybe that will help. . . ."

I sighed. "But I'm understanding people, too. I can tell what they . . . well, I don't know exactly. I can *hear* them in some way. And that's the thing: I might hear something from you, like how you really feel about me."

"Oh," said Nick. I was walking very fast, but he kept up. No matter how fast I walked, he stayed right with me. "I don't care if you do. You must know anyway. I totally like you. I mean . . . I know things are getting awfully weird."

I stopped walking. I looked away from him. Then I turned and threw my arms around him.

"Whoa," he said. "Emily."

I wanted to cry, I liked him so much, and when we hugged I could feel he was telling the truth. His whole being was saying it. He wanted to be with me, and help me, and protect me any way he could.

"Hey," said Nick, pulling away. He looked at his hands and down at his body. "Did you feel that? Just now? It was like a little shock or something."

"I know; that's part of it," I said. "It goes away. I just have a lot of it right now."

"Where does it come from?"

"I don't know exactly," I said, touching his arm. "But you should go back now. Stay with Sheila. I'll call you guys when it's time. Can you get a car?"

"Of course," he said. "We'll steal one if we have to." He was watching my hand, where it touched him.

"Okay," I said, releasing him.

"No, wait, do that again; touch me again," he said.

"No. It's not good for you. I have to go. Tell Sheila we'll call you guys."

47

The food must have helped, I realized as I walked down the road to my dad's house. Ever since Steve and Dave had been eating, the dreams had gotten stronger, the warm feelings had gotten stronger, the connection between the people who had been around them had gotten stronger. Even people like Sheila and Nick were getting swept into it. It was like a network now, of communication, of energy, of a strange loyalty that spread to everyone who came into contact with Steve and Dave.

But would it be enough?

I came around the corner of my road. I felt a sense of alarm of some sort, from the birds maybe. But when I looked up into the trees there was nothing. I looked into the underbrush. Maybe a cat was chasing mice. But there were no cats. There were no mice.

Then something happened in my brain and I ran to the side of the road and threw myself into the bushes. I had no idea why I did it, but not two seconds later a black sedan came roaring down the road, bouncing on the bumps and potholes and leaving a thick cloud of summer dust behind it. A few moments later another black sedan did the same thing, this one with a police light flashing from inside, on the dashboard. They were the Feds. I knew it. They were hunting down Dave and Steve.

I waited a moment, after they passed, then crawled from my hiding place and checked the road. Nick was right; it would be better if I were a boy. They were better at running and hiding. But not *that much* better.

I looked both ways. The coast was clear, so I sprinted back to the main road, crossed it, and dove into the bushes again. I heard a helicopter overhead. I thought about my dad. I thought about Steve and Dave. I tried to search my thoughts in case they were trying to tell me something. But I couldn't hear anything, not in the air or inside my own brain.

I remembered a path through the woods that led eventually to the lake behind Reese's house. I started pushing through the brush and sticks in that direction. It was tough going, but I found the trail. I could walk easier once I was on it, but now it was getting dark. I started to get scared.

I also noticed I was scaring the creatures around me. The birds were upset. And other things, things down by my feet. I tried to communicate back to them: *I am alone and in trouble. I am not here to hurt you. Help me find my way.*

It was like a little prayer. I don't know if anything "heard" me, or understood what I was saying, but it made me feel better, and it gave me something to think about.

The next thing I knew, I was at the lake.

48

At dusk the lake looked particularly beautiful. It was still and calm, and the last of the daylight gave it a silvery sheen. Bugs silently swarmed in spots along the bank. Fish jumped every few seconds. Different kinds of birds gathered, some skimming along the surface for bugs, others waiting in trees or swooping down from high above to catch a fish. The best thing was, they were all linked together, all living things were, all life on Earth was like a big fuzzy moss that covered the surface of the planet. Was there really any difference between a blade of grass and a person? Or a fish and a flower? Maybe that's what the dreams were about, because the dreams were always about water and the sun. And weren't those the two things that all life came from? And wasn't the bliss of the dreams maybe the bliss of all life on Earth, of all life period, and how everything was connected to everything else, and the joy that harmony created?

Communication. That was the key. That was why Steve and Dave were so different from us. Because they had achieved total communication with all living things. They were fully integrated, while we humans were still on the outside looking in.

It was an interesting thought, but I had to focus on more immediate problems. I was almost to Reese's house. If the Feds were at my house, wouldn't they be at Reese's, too? I crept quietly along the bank. As I got closer to Reese's boathouse I stopped and listened. I could feel something bad. The boathouse was back in the trees, but I could see the little dock by the water. There appeared to be no one there. There appeared to be total silence and calm. But I knew it wasn't right. I stayed where I was. I listened. I watched.

Then something moved. It was an arm . . . it was an arm with a black sleeve on it . . . it was an arm . . . moving up to a face . . . *duh*—it was a man in a suit eating a candy bar. He was standing in the bushes. It was the Feds; they were at Reese's, hiding, waiting to see who might show up. Which meant Dave and Steve either were caught or had escaped. I looked around the lake. About a hundred yards in the other direction I saw a large rowboat upside down on the bank. There was something about it. Was it . . . *calling me?*

I crept carefully through the woods in that direction. I moved very slowly. By the time I got to the boat it was completely dark, which could only help.

I stayed hidden in the trees. I got as close as I could and whispered to the boat's hull, "Dave? Steve?"

"Honey," came a voice. It was my dad! My sixty-two-year-old dad was hiding under a rowboat!

"Dad?" I said.

The boat shifted. An eye peeked out from under it.

"Who's under there?" I said.

"All of us," said Steve.

"Reese, too?"

"Yes."

"Honey, is it safe yet?" asked my dad's voice. "Are those men still over at the Ridgleys'?"

"Yeah, I saw them in the bushes," I whispered. "They're not very good hiders. One guy was eating a candy bar."

"Our federal government at work," mumbled my dad from under the boat. The federal government was one of his favorite complaints.

"Can we get out, without being seen?" said Steve.

"I think so," I said.

They tilted the boat a little to one side and Steve slid out from under it. He stayed low to the ground and hurried to where I was, behind a tree. Dave came next, while Steve and I watched the Ridgleys'. Then my dad. He looked great and he wasn't limping. Finally Reese crawled out. She didn't look so good. She stumbled and fell and when she stood she had trouble keeping her balance. I ran forward and grabbed her and led her into the trees. She kept leaning to one side. At least she was awake, though.

I led her behind a tree. She was dressed funny; Steve

and Dave had probably dressed her. She was also dirty from lying on the ground. "Are you okay?" I whispered.

She nodded that she was. "Just feel a little wobbly. . . . "

She lifted her head and that's when I saw her eyes. They were electric. They shone. They were like blue crystals or blue skies or blue oceans as deep and endless as you could imagine.

"What?" she said. "What are you looking at? Do I have dirt on my face?"

"A little," I said, I pretended to brush something off her forehead with my hand.

We crawled deeper into the woods. We went slowly, a few feet at a time. It was so dark now, you couldn't see anything. I almost got poked in the eye with a stick.

Eventually we found the main road. But what then? As we crept through the trees toward it, a car came speeding by. We all dove for cover, but it was just an SUV, probably tourists. I would have called Nick and Sheila, but none of us had a phone. Of course, if my stupid parents had given me a cell phone, like every other sixteen-year-old girl had . . . but I couldn't think about that now. Steve and Dave crawled over to where my dad was. They talked and weighed their options.

Then I heard a Metallica song. It was so loud it was booming through the forest. It was coming nearer, too. It was Harold and Carl; I could see their truck. I could see Carl watching out the window. *They were looking for us.*

I knew I wouldn't be able to shout over their stereo, so I scrambled toward the road. I dug at my feet for something to throw. I found a rock. As the truck passed, I threw the rock as hard as I could. By some miracle it reached the truck and bounced off the hood. Harold immediately hit the brakes. The stereo went off.

"Harold, it's us!" I hissed.

Behind me, Reese, my dad, Dave, and Steve all struggled through the brush to the road. Harold and Carl both hopped out of the truck. Carl helped my dad while Harold unfolded a tarp in the back of his truck. As fast as we could, we all crawled under it. He arranged us beneath it and tied it down.

"Take us to New Branford," Steve told Harold.

"You got it," said Harold.

Twenty minutes later we were safely out of town. But it was horrible under the tarp; you could barely breathe and whenever there was the slightest bump you bounced up and down on the hard metal. Harold stopped at a strip mall so we could get some air. Carl had a cell phone, so I immediately called Nick and Sheila. We didn't have an exact plan yet, but I told them I'd call and we'd all meet in New Branford the next day.

We didn't go all the way to New Branford that night. Instead we stopped and slept in an old barn Harold knew about. I think it was a hangout for him and his local friends. There was a car seat with cigarette burns in it and old beer bottles and some blankets in the hay bales where they probably made out with their local girlfriends.

Reese and I crawled into the hay and fell asleep so fast, I didn't even remember lying down. I had some dreams; Reese did, too, but they seemed less than usual. It was good, I guess. We didn't need any more euphoria; we needed sleep.

The next morning we ate breakfast in a diner and proceeded to New Branford. My dad and I rode in the front of the pickup with Steve and Harold. When we arrived, my dad had Harold drive up the road to the research facility, to see what we could learn by acting like casual visitors.

A cold breeze had started that morning. That was very unusual in July. Harold had to roll up his window. He even turned on his heater. The Metallica cassette was still playing on the stereo, very quietly now.

We drove until we came to a makeshift traffic stop. A police car and two unmarked sedans blocked the road. Harold slowed to a stop as the two cops in uniform got out of their car and approached us. My dad rolled down his window and greeted them through the passenger window. "Hello, Officers; what's going on?"

"We have a restricted-access situation here. We're not letting anyone into the facility at this time."

"Well, I'm Professor Dalton, and this is my daughter. I have actually spoken with Dr. Leonard—"

"Doesn't matter, sir; no one goes in. No one goes out. It's a special situation."

"Oh, I see."

"We'll need you to turn your vehicle around and—," the cop started to say, but his hat blew off. He ran after it. The wind was suddenly blowing hard. I looked into the back of the pickup; the tarp was holding okay, but the wind was cold and it felt like it might rain.

"Weird weather," said the policeman when he returned to the window. "Like I said, we'll need you to turn the vehicle around."

Harold shifted the truck into reverse. I watched one of the officers struggle to put on a rain poncho. The hood blew up in his face.

Big drops of rain began to hit our windshield. Harold turned the truck around and drove back to the town.

A couple miles from the research facility we found an abandoned gas station and parked under the awning. Carl, Dave, and Reese got out of the back. Nick and Sheila called, and I directed them to where we were. An hour later they pulled in behind us.

Everyone stood around the pickup truck. It was raining, the wind was blowing hard, and sheets of water would periodically slap down onto the pavement. My dad shivered in the sudden cold. He turned to Steve. "You're creating this weather, aren't you?"

Everyone watched Steve. We had all noticed the weird weather. Nick and Sheila were putting on sweatshirts.

Steve shook his head. "We are not nearly so powerful."

My dad thought for a moment. "What about your friends? The others, still in the ocean? Are they doing it?"

"It is not important," said Steve, turning away. But my dad was right. Of course they were doing it.

50

For the rest of the afternoon Steve, Dave, and my dad fine-tuned their plan. Basically, it was this: Nick and Sheila would buy some beer and act like teenagers looking for a party. They would approach the front entrance, and when they got stopped they would become belligerent, cause a scene, act drunk, whatever would distract the guards there.

Harold, Carl, Reese, and I would do the same thing at the back entrance, at the same time.

Steve, Dave, and my dad (since my dad knew the facility) would hike through the woods and while we were creating our simultaneous distraction sneak in a side entrance.

We had three cell phones now, so we could all talk to

one another. If something went wrong or we had to retreat, we would all meet back at the abandoned gas station an hour after we started.

Everyone liked the plan, but I kept wondering how they were going to get the white blob out of the place. My dad said the government scientists were keeping it in an oxygenated tank of seawater, refrigerated to the exact temperature of the bottom of the Atlantic, in hopes that it would return to its normal state—whatever that was. But how were Steve and Dave going to carry a huge tank of oxygenated water out of the highly-guarded compound?

I didn't know. I trusted my dad. I trusted Dave and Steve. I also had to trust Harold and Carl. I felt less comfortable about that. As we waited near the back entrance they pulled a bottle of whiskey from under the seat. They began drinking from it and spilling it around the cab so we would smell intoxicated.

"Don't get it on me," I said.

"You heard your dad," said Harold. "We're supposed to be drunk."

After that, we listened to Metallica and waited for everyone to get in position. It was cold and windy, and unfortunately, Harold's heater didn't really work. Harold and Carl began drinking the whiskey for warmth.

"Give us some; we're cold, too," said Reese after they had had several slugs. Harold handed it over.

"Here, sit close; it'll warm you up," said Carl.

"Get away from me," said Reese.

"Hey, you're going to be my girlfriend for two weeks after this," joked Harold. "You'd better be nice."

At that moment Carl, who had not looked closely at Reese all day, glanced into her face. He recoiled slightly. "Dude, what's up with your eyes?" he said.

"I'm not a *dude,*" said Reese, grabbing the whiskey away from him.

"No, but your—"

"Nothing's wrong with my eyes," said Reese. She drank a little of the whiskey. "Is there something wrong with my eyes?" she asked me.

I looked into them. They were like before, glowing, electric, with a blueness and a depthless quality that was hard not to notice.

"What?" she said to me. "What's wrong with them?" She sat forward and turned the rearview mirror so she could see herself. Harold turned on the cab light for her. She looked. She saw what Carl had seen. She looked at me with alarm. "My eyes . . . why are they glowing like that?" She tilted her head at different angles. "Turn off the light, Harold," she said. She continued to look. "What's wrong with them? Jesus, *what's happened to me!*"

"It's the energy," I said quietly.

"What energy? What are you talking about?"

"The energy that Steve and Dave give off. The thing that makes you feel good. Do you remember what you did last night?"

"No, what did I do last night?" she asked me. "Didn't I . . . sleep with you?"

I shook my head.

"What did I do? Tell me."

"You slept with Dave," I said. "Right up against him."

"I knew it," snorted Harold with disgust.

"I did not," said Reese. "How could I? How could I not remember?"

"You guys are too weird," said Carl.

"Will they stay like this?" said Reese, looking back in the mirror. "My eyes can't stay like this. Can they?"

"Maybe you could get contacts," said Carl.

"It'll probably wear off," I said. "It all wears off eventually."

"It looks kind of cool," offered Harold.

"It looks kind of . . . scary," said Carl.

Part FIVE

(Associated Press) WASHINGTON, D.C. — Officials from the U.S. Navy announced today that radiation levels in the North Atlantic have lowered in recent days and soon the area will return to normal.

Radiation levels had been considered dangerously high because of a leaking nuclear missile lost in the area in early June. Scientists believe the missing Baldwin "Hellfire" missile is at the bottom of MacKenzie's Crevice, a deep canyon on the ocean floor.

Several environmental groups and the Canadian Maritime Council have insisted that the U.S. Navy and other officials have attempted to cover up details of the incident.

A spokesman from Greenpeace International was quoted as saying: "The dissipation of the radioactivity does not mean that this eco-disaster is over. It means it is spreading. Every ocean on Earth will ultimately be affected by this, just as every ocean is affected by all the deadly toxins that are released into the oceans every day."

A Navy spokesman declined to comment.

51

My cell phone rang. It was my dad. "Go in thirty seconds. And Emily, above all, be careful. Just make a nuisance of yourself. Don't do anything risky."

"Okay, Dad, you be careful, too. Please please please be careful. I love you more than anything."

"Okay, honey."

I hung up. "They say to go in thirty seconds," I told Harold.

He nodded. Everyone got quiet. We all looked through the rain-blurred windshield at the road ahead.

"Ten seconds," I said, watching the time on the cell phone.

Harold counted silently to ten and took a deep breath.

He shifted the pickup into drive. He'd been waiting for this moment his whole life.

We drove slowly up the little road that was the back entrance. We came around some trees and there was the roadblock, as expected. It was the same as in front: two police cars, two sedans, six or seven policemen. A yellow and white wood barricade blocked the narrow access road.

As happened before, several people got out of their cars to confront us. Two uniformed policemen came forward. "Stop please," said the first one as Harold rolled down his window.

"Hey, dude," said Harold. "Wudup? Why ya blocking my road?"

The cop eyed him suspiciously. "This is private property," said the cop. "We're going to have to ask you—"

"Private property?" sneered Harold. "Since when? This is the research place; we come up here all the time—"

The cop got a call on his radio. He turned away from Harold and answered it. A look of concern flashed over the cop's face. Maybe Nick and Sheila had already done something. Another cop approached the passenger side. He gripped his hat so it wouldn't blow off. A third cop, in an orange raincoat, positioned himself in front of the barricade. He was getting pounded by the wind and the rain and he wasn't enjoying it.

The first cop listened to his radio while Harold continued his banter. "You can't block off a road just because you feel like it," he said. "How do I know you're real cops anyway? I've never seen you before. You got an ID?" He revved the engine of the pickup truck and stared at the cop directly in front of us. That cop became nervous and discreetly moved to one side.

Meanwhile the second cop, on Carl's side, got a call on his radio. They were both having trouble hearing in the wind. Finally, another man, in plainclothes, got out of a black sedan and approached our truck. This man wore tinted sunglasses and a radio headset. He looked far more serious than the others, like he knew how to handle punks like Harold.

But Harold was not going to be handled. Not today. He smiled at the man, revved the engine, and slammed the gas pedal to the floor.

The truck leapt forward. The policemen scattered. We crashed through the wood barricade, bounced off the back of a police car, and were suddenly driving unobstructed up the access road toward the research facility.

"Wah-hoo!" shrieked Harold.

"Yeee-hahhhh!" said Carl, looking back at the confusion we had left in our wake. *"Suckas!"* he cried. "You just got *punked*!"

"But you guys!" I shouted. "We're not supposed to go inside. We're just supposed to create a distraction! *Away* from the facility."

"Hey, I can do that," said Harold, and he swerved the pickup truck to the right.

We bounced over the curb and onto the wet grass beside the access road. There was a huge groomed lawn all around the buildings and now we bounced and skidded across it. I looked back. Some of the cops were running up the lawn in our direction. The two police cars backed out of their places and turned up the long driveway. They both bumped violently over the curb and came speeding at us. They seemed to float across the sea of grass, their sirens shrieking, their lights flashing.

"Hell-o!" screamed Harold over the noise. He was steering the truck along the longest stretch of the lawn. We were bouncing and skidding and barely under control. The speedometer was at forty miles an hour, but the police were still catching up.

When they were almost on us, Harold slammed on the brakes. One of the cop cars zoomed past on the right. Harold jerked the truck hard to the left, and the other cop car, which was beside us, swerved wildly and skidded sideways. Grass and sod went flying.

"Ahhh!" I screamed. "Harold! Be careful! Don't hit anyone!"

This was a real danger, as the cops on foot were now running across the lawn with their guns drawn. Harold was not afraid. He spun the pickup around and drove directly at one of the policemen on foot. The cop scrambled to get out of the way. He slipped in the wet grass; Harold jerked the truck hard to the right and just missed him.

"Harold! Stop it! They're going to shoot us!" I cried.

"They ain't shootin' nobody!" said Harold. The two unmarked sedans had been slow to join the chase. Now they were coming right at us. Harold played chicken with them: steering straight ahead and gaining speed. Reese screamed. I turned away. Both sedans swerved violently to either side.

"Yeooowww!" shrieked Carl.

Once the sedans were behind us, there was no one left in front of us. All the cars were on the lawn, the cops, too, and the once heavily-guarded driveway was now wide open. Harold steered the truck toward it. We skidded and slid through the grass, bounced back onto the access road, and escaped through the broken barricade.

52

At the exact moment we took off across the lawn, Steve, Dave, and my dad had positioned themselves in the woods across from a lightly-guarded side entrance. Here there was only one security guard. As my dad had hoped, when this lonely guard heard about the car chase on his radio, he couldn't resist running to the front of the building to have a look. Steve, Dave, and my dad bolted for the door and were inside in seconds.

Inside, my dad found a supply closet and got everyone a white lab coat. Thus disguised, they made their way through the various buildings and connecting hallways to the lab where the organism was. The facility, which was usually full of researchers and students, was practically deserted. The Feds had become so baffled by the organism, and so afraid of it, they had declared the site off-limits until someone in Washington could decide what to do. This helped immensely. Steve and Dave barely had to hide, and my father, with his white hair and professorial demeanor, easily nodded his way past the few people they encountered.

The actual laboratory posed a more serious problem. There were several guards sitting around a desk outside the lab door. My dad huddled with Steve and Dave. What could they do about the guards? Was there anything Steve and Dave could do, with their ability to manipulate molecular structure? My dad tried to remember his time teaching there; was there anything they could use?

Then he got an idea. . . .

Meanwhile, Harold careened down the access road and skidded wildly onto the main road. "Oh my god!" shouted Reese. "We did it! We totally escaped!"

Harold focused on the road. He was going fifty through the curves. The pickup swerved from side to side. "I say we go to the front entrance and do the same thing," he said.

"We don't need to," I said. "Nick is there."

"Yeah, but he's Australian," said Harold. "Australians can't drive."

"She's right," said Carl, checking the road behind us. "We did our part. Let's get out of here."

"But what if they need more time?" I said. Our little joyride had barely taken ten minutes. I pulled out the cell phone to call my dad. It was already ringing.

"Shhhhh!" I said to everyone. I pushed the button and listened.

It wasn't my dad; it was Sheila. She was screaming hysterically. "They shot Nick!" she wailed. "Someone help us! Please! Help! Someone! They shot Nick. He's bleeding. He's *dying* . . . "

Everyone in the pickup stared down at the cell phone. "Oh my god," whispered Reese. "Now what do we do?"

53

Deep inside the main building of the research facility, no one knew anything about shots being fired. The security people guarding the secured special projects lab were drinking coffee and listening to the weather report on the news radio station. The Red Sox game was going to be canceled, it sounded like. They sat at a small table, with chairs, and grumbled about the strange weather.

Then a man in an orange protective suit appeared at the end of the hall. The group of them stopped talking to watch the man walk toward them. The orange jumpsuit had the words HAZ MAT stamped across the front; it had airtight boots and a sealed anticontamination helmet that looked like a bug's head. The man also carried a Geiger counter, the old kind, which were only used for teaching nowadays. But the guards didn't know that. They had seen Geiger counters on TV. They knew what they measured.

The guards watched as this unidentified man swept its detector wand back and forth. The shoe-box-sized machine he held in his other hand clicked noisily. As the man came closer to the main lab, the clicking increased.

The guards were stunned into silence by this strange sight. Finally one spoke: "Excuse me, sir; this area is restricted. Unless you have authorization—"

The orange suit pointed the detector wand directly at the lab door. The Geiger counter clicked more rapidly.

"Uh, excuse me," said the same guard. He stepped forward. "If you could identify yourself?"

The man in the HAZ MAT suit did not identify himself. He pointed the wand at the man's belt buckle. The Geiger counter clicked wildly.

"Does that mean what I think it means?" one of the other guards whispered.

"It means radiation," said another.

"It must be that blob thing in the lab," said a third guard.

"Hey, nobody said the thing was *radioactive.*"

"It figures they wouldn't tell us."

"We're supposed to get paid extra for that."

"Yeah, hazardous duty."

"Hey! A little help here?" said the guy who's belt buckle was producing the worst of the clicking.

The other guards ignored him. "Jesus, I can't get *irradiated.* I wanna have kids."

"Me, too."

"My wife will kill me."

The orange suit continued to point the detector wand. When he aimed it directly at the four guards, the little box clicked as if they were a toxic-waste dump.

The one who wanted to have kids ran first. He was followed by the one whose wife was going to kill him. In a few seconds they were all gone. The hall was clear. The lab was unguarded.

Steve tore off the orange suit. He, Dave, and my dad ran to the laboratory entrance. The door was locked, but the guards had conveniently left the keys on the desk. My dad unlocked the door, and the three of them burst into the room.

It was a large, high-ceilinged room, crowded with sophisticated electronic equipment. Wires and tubes hung from scaffolds and metal platforms. In the middle of it, surrounded by computers and monitors, was an enormous forty-thousand-gallon oxygenated water tank. It was illuminated by spotlights. Bubbles streamed up the inside of the tank like a giant aquarium.

There was just one problem: There was nothing in it. It was completely empty.

"I don't understand," said my father. "This should be it. Unless there's another tank."

"No, this is it," said Dave.

"He was here," said Steve. He walked around the tank. "He was here a day ago."

"How do you know?"

"He was awake. He was communicating with us. Or trying to. . . ."

"Well, communicate with him now," said my father. "We have to find him. We don't have much time."

Steve shook his head.

"What?" said my dad. "What is it?"

"We've lost him. We can't hear him anymore," said Steve.

"Our powers of communication are fading very quickly now," said Dave.

"So what do we do?" asked my dad. "How do we find him?"

The three of them stood around the tank, unsure of what to do. Then my dad saw the emergency door exit. He ran to it. It had been opened. He could tell because of a special seal that had been broken.

"Could he have gotten out of the tank on his own?" asked my father. "And escaped?"

Steve and Dave weren't sure. But they were definitely going to find out.

54

"Sheila! Where are you?" I yelled into the phone. Harold was still swerving through the curves.

"We're on the road!" she answered. "Going back to town. Oh my god! Nick's bleeding all over!"

"Is he awake?"

"*No, he's not awake!*" she screamed. "He's been shot! He's dying. He's going to die!"

"Go to the gas station!" I said as loud as I could. "We'll get Dave and Steve. Do you hear me? *Go to the gas station*!" I listened for a response, but she was crying hysterically. I hung up. I dialed my father.

"Emily," he said. "What is it?"

"Dad!" I shrieked. "They shot Nick. Sheila's got him in her car. Dad! You have to get Steve and Dave!"

"Where's Sheila?"

"She's going back to the gas station."

"Where are you?"

"We're on the main road. Heading toward town."

Suddenly Harold slammed on the brakes. Everyone crashed forward. I could barely hang on to the phone.

"Tell your dad we'll meet him where we dropped him off," shouted Harold. "We'll be there in thirty seconds."

"Dad," I screamed into the phone. "Did you hear that? Meet us where we dropped you off!"

Harold whipped the truck around. A moment later we were going sixty again, in the opposite direction.

"Emily," said my dad, through a crackle of static. "We've lost the organism. It's not here. And Steve and Dave, something's happening to them; they're losing their powers—"

A cop car suddenly appeared. It was coming straight at us. Harold slammed on the brakes. Everyone crashed forward. The cop car, to avoid hitting us, skidded sideways off the road and thudded into the ditch.

The cell phone fell to the floor. I picked it up. It was off. I turned it back on and frantically dialed my father again. The pickup truck roared forward so violently I knocked heads with Reese and dropped the phone again. It bounced under the seat. Reese crawled onto the floor, grabbed it, and jammed it into my hands.

I dialed. The phone wouldn't stay on. I tried again. It still wouldn't stay on. Then I saw: the back of it was broken.

Another police car came flying around the corner straight at us. Harold swerved again. We crashed to the side. The police car missed us by inches and Harold floored it again. We were all thrown backward.

"What did he say?" shouted Harold over the noise of the engine.

"I don't know," I said. "The phone is broken."

I watched out the front as Harold sped past the access road. We were now heading toward the back of the facility, to the place we'd dropped off Steve and Dave and my dad.

There was no one chasing us now. Everyone was quiet as the truck sped along the wet road at seventy miles an hour.

Then it occurred to me: What if Steve and Dave didn't come? Why would they? Wouldn't they look for their friend first? Wasn't that what this was all about?

What had I done? I suddenly thought. Steve and Dave didn't really care about us. We had been brainwashed. We had been tricked. And now Nick was going to die and it was my fault! A sudden sob leapt out of my chest. I gripped the dashboard, lowered my head. I thought I was going to die; I wanted to die.

Reese yanked me up. We were at the place. In front of us, standing in the road, soaked and muddy, were my father . . . and Dave.

55

Oh my god, and this was the strangest part—and the luckiest, for us.

While all this other stuff was happening, Luke and Jimmy were back in South Point, hanging out in their police car, watching the rain and listening to their police scanner. They heard a couple unusual things on the radio from New Branford and they were bored and Jimmy used to go to high school there, so they decided to go for a drive.

When they arrived in New Branford, the rain and wind had emptied Main Street. There were no tourists, no girls, no sign of whatever action they had heard on the radio. They cruised the arcade, the Galaxy Burger. They checked out Coffee Haus, which was where the younger crowd tended to hang out in bad weather. That's when Jimmy spotted a strange-looking man, dressed in what looked like a janitor's uniform, sitting on a bench across from Coffee Haus. Luke saw him, too.

They ignored him and drove down Main Street again. Luke called in to his uncle, who was in South Point. They were about to leave when Jimmy saw a girl in a rain slicker coming out of Coffee Haus. "Dude, that's Marnie Krauss," he said to Luke. "I went to high school with her. Pull over a sec."

Luke eased the squad card to the curb.

"Hey, Marnie, what's up?"

"Oh. Hey, Jimmy," said the girl. She was obviously not so thrilled to see him. "What's up with you?"

"Just, you know, doing some police work," said Jimmy.

"What, driving around looking for girls?"

"No, for real," said Jimmy, a little embarrassed. "I'm a cop now. I mean, I sort of am. This is Luke. He's a deputy in South Point. We're checking on some stuff for the Feds."

"Why don't you check out that weird guy sitting on that bench?" she said.

Jimmy and Luke both looked at the guy on the bench. He was the same guy they had noticed before, with the badly fitting janitor uniform. "Why? What's up with him?"

"He's been sitting there for hours," said Marnie. "He looks kinda messed up. He must be freezing."

"Yeah?" said Jimmy, turning back to Marnie. He smiled at her. "You're looking good. What you been up to lately?"

Marnie was not interested in Jimmy. She continued to watch the guy on the bench. "My friend tried to talk to him," she said. "She said he talked gibberish and baby talk and stuff."

Jimmy glanced back at the guy. "Yeah? I mean, we're kind of busy, but I guess we could check it out."

"You should," said Marnie, pulling the hood of her rain slicker over her head. "Gotta go. See you, later."

56

Once we'd picked up Dave and my dad in the pickup, Harold floored it back to the gas station. We were going faster than I had ever ridden in a car. We had to. Nick was dying.

In minutes we were bouncing into the back parking lot of the gas station. Sheila was there, crouched by the passenger side of her car, desperately trying to help Nick. Dave and my dad jumped out to help. Nick was passed out in the passenger seat. You could see the blood. You could see the white ghostliness in his face. Another sob forced its way through my chest. Reese grabbed me and pulled me away. "Don't watch," she said. "Come over here."

Harold wanted to help, but my dad moved everyone

away so Dave could heal Nick. Sheila followed Reese and me. She was crying hysterically. She wanted to call 911, but Reese took the phone away from her. "Dave can save him," said Reese.

"But what if he can't?" Sheila moaned to me. I pulled her close to me and hugged her. Reese grabbed us both and we all hugged and cried as the rain poured down around us.

"I saw him heal that other guy," I heard Harold tell Carl. "They start to glow and stuff."

But whatever Dave had done that time was not working so well now. I could tell by the way my dad began frantically yelling for stuff. First he wanted our T-shirts, or any clean clothes we had on. Then he needed water. We brought it to him in water bottles. I could barely look when I handed it to him. Nick looked worse than ever. . . .

At that same moment, back in New Branford, Luke steered the squad car toward the guy on the bench.

"Marnie was sorta into me, didn't you think?" Jimmy said as they approached him.

"No," said Luke.

"Yeah, but you could tell she was sorta impressed and stuff, right?"

Luke said nothing. He pulled in front of the bench. The strange man looked about twenty-five. He was soaked to the skin. He didn't act cold, though. He wasn't shivering; he seemed utterly oblivious to the harsh weather.

Luke eased to a stop.

"What do we do with this dude?" asked Jimmy.

"Talk to him."

Jimmy frowned. The man was on his side of the car. Jimmy rolled down his window. "Hey, you," he called from the car. "Why doncha get outta the rain?"

The young man lifted his head and slowly turned to face the police car. "Look at this guy," Jimmy whispered to Luke. "What drugs is he on?"

"Ask him where he's staying," said Luke.

"Hey!" Jimmy addressed the man. "Where you staying?"

The man didn't answer.

"Jeez," said Jimmy to himself. "What's wrong with people? Doesn't he know we're cops?"

Luke had not been interested in this person before. Now he watched him closely. There was something not right about his face. And yet there was something familiar about his movements.

"Dude, I'm a *cop,*" Jimmy called to the man. "I'm asking you a question. Where are you from? Hello? Speak English?"

The man moved his mouth. A strange word came out that sounded like, "Yah."

"This guy's high," Jimmy said to Luke.

Luke wasn't listening. He picked up his cell phone. He began to look through his numbers.

"Listen," said Jimmy, addressing the stranger one last time. "If you make me get out of this car I'm going to be pissed. And you don't want to see me pissed."

The man did not move.

"I give up," said Jimmy. He sat back in his seat. Luke

had punched in a number and was holding his cell phone to his ear. "Who ya callin'?" asked Jimmy.

"Professor Dalton."

"What are you calling him for?"

"Hello? . . . Who's this?" said Luke into his phone. "Emily? . . . Hey. Listen, you know those exchange students you were hanging out with? How many were there? . . . Yeah? You're missing one? Well, I may have found your man."

57

I don't remember what I said back exactly. Something like: "Luke, I know a lot of weird stuff is happening. But if you could bring that guy to us, everything will work out, I swear."

I waited a moment for Luke to respond.

"Yeah, all right," he said.

But even with Luke on his way, no one was relaxing at the gas station. Nick was getting worse. Sheila was completely hysterical. Harold and Carl were sitting dejectedly in their truck, adding up all the laws they had broken. Steve had finally appeared. He had stayed behind to search the grounds of the research facility. He had found nothing and then stolen a Toyota Corolla, which he didn't know how to drive and now crashed into some trash cans because he didn't know how to put it into park. Steve was now helping with Nick, but even with the two of them, their powers were so weak they could barely keep Nick alive.

Thank god for Luke. I had barely hung up with him when his squad car came tearing into the gas station. Though I hadn't explained much on the phone, he and Jimmy seemed to understand what was happening—maybe they remembered the thicket. They stopped their car next to Sheila's and quickly pulled the third "exchange student" out of the backseat. Everyone gasped at the sight of him. He barely looked human. There was a weird plastic quality to his face. He didn't seem able to speak, or even to see.

Luke and Jimmy hopped back in their car and took off—they didn't know what we were doing and they didn't want to know.

Steve and Dave helped their friend steady himself. They guided him to Nick. My dad moved everyone else away.

The rest of us waited. We didn't have to wait long. It took thirty seconds to heal Nick. The "exchange student" was brand-new; he had all his communication powers; he had powers coming out his ears.

Steve named the new guy Mike. Steve wasn't terribly creative when it came to naming people. Once Nick was safe again, we all stood for a moment in the rain, staring at Mike. He was tall and dressed in janitor clothes that were too small and obviously stolen. His hands didn't seem the right size for his body, and he had the same featureless quality in his face that Steve and Dave had when we first met them. Steve and Dave, I realized, had hardened in the time we had known them. They did not change anymore. They had become human, stuck inside their formed bodies like the rest of us.

My dad interrupted everyone to remind us we had to get out of New Branford. The police might still be looking for us. Somebody surely would be.

That's what we did. All the young people got in Sheila's car with Nick, who was moved to the backseat. My dad drove Harold's pickup with Steve, Dave, and Mike inside the cab. The two cars pulled onto the road and we began our attempted escape.

I was sure we would get caught. Every turn I waited for the police sirens to start. None did. My dad drove right through downtown New Branford and then onto Route 6. We drove north, away from South Point. We drove for an hour, slowly, carefully. It was still pouring down rain and now completely dark. My dad finally pulled into a solitary motel called the Sea View. It was off the main road and overlooked the ocean.

We parked the pickup and the car on the beach side lot, where they couldn't be seen from the road. We checked into two connected rooms, moved Nick in, and settled ourselves in for the night.

Part SIX

58

"They're the ultimate communicators," my dad said. "We communicate with speech and visual cues, which is a very primitive level. They communicate on every level, cellular, molecular, telekinetic even. . . . And they can influence other organisms to do the same."

I nodded. I watched him pack his pipe. We were sitting on a bench outside our room. In front of us, in the warm night, we could see the great wide ocean.

"I could hear things for a while," I told him, "or not *hear* exactly, but I could sense what different animals were saying. And people, too. And I knew things about them."

"They are the most perfect conductors of information I can imagine," said my dad, lighting his pipe. "In their natural state, they literally monitor the entire planet."

"They're like God, listening to our prayers," I said.

"Our prayers and our curses and every other noise we make," said my dad. "And at the same time they do nothing themselves. They want nothing. They need nothing."

"But they don't create anything, either," I said.

"Ah, but is creation necessary?" said my father. "Do we really need to build and change and process everything? Maybe we don't. They don't. They're beyond it."

"Wouldn't that be boring, though?"

"To us. Obviously not to them. Think about monks who sit in silent meditation for days at a time; they're not bored. They become explorers of internal worlds. They experience all sorts of different sensations, different planes of consciousness."

"You think that's what the aliens do?" I said.

"It seems possible," said my father. "Hidden down there, perfectly silent, perfectly still, and yet somehow connecting to all the different energies of the Earth . . ." My father smoked his pipe. "It's really a remarkable model. We're so activity oriented. The idea that these beings have evolved in an opposite direction . . ."

I watched the waves roll in. I watched my dad smoke. "I am kind of jealous that they live forever," I said.

"That part is certainly alien to us," said my dad.

"Do you wish you could live forever?"

My father stared at the ocean. "As a scientist I do. Of course I do. But as a person, well, we're not built to last forever.

"Steve says humans don't die; they just get recycled."

My dad laughed. "They know more about us than we know about ourselves."

I nodded. My dad was such a good teacher. He had a way of bringing things into focus and at the same time forcing you to let your mind wander. It made you want to be his student. No wonder my mother fell in love with him.

Later, Nick woke up. He didn't say anything; he just sat there blinking at us. Carl and Harold drove to a pizza place up the road and came back with three large pizzas. We practically ripped open the boxes, we were so hungry.

Steve and Dave and Mike wouldn't have any, though. They said they couldn't; they needed to empty themselves.

Everyone stared at Steve when he said that. My dad asked if they would be returning to the ocean soon. Steve nodded. Naturally, I didn't want them to go anywhere, none of us did, but we were so hungry all we could do was eat.

After the pizza, people got sleepy. Sheila crawled onto the bed with her brother, Nick, and dozed off and began to snore softly. Reese fell asleep on the floor beside Nick's bed with a blanket over her. Steve, Dave, and Mike went into the other room with my dad. He never got tired of talking to them and asking them questions.

Harold slept in his clothes on the other bed with Carl curled up beside him. I was the last of the young people still awake. I got a blanket and lay on the floor next to Reese. I was close enough to the wall that I could hear my dad and Steve still talking. I tried to stay awake and listen. But it was no use. I was so tired. And the dreams were waiting for me; I could feel them. Finally I closed my eyes and drifted off to sleep.

That night was the most intense of all the dream nights. Slowly, gradually, the darkness of sleep was illuminated by a soft white light. As the whiteness grew stronger, I was lifted into the air, where I began to float through pulsing liquid clouds of warmth and light and pure sensation. Each new cloud had a different quality: perfect warmth, perfect light, perfect understanding. I got the sense that everyone else in the room was having the dreams, too. The fact that we were all together and that Steve and Dave, and now Mike, were there, it compounded everything. It was like beyond dreaming, beyond sleeping; it was like going to a different dimension.

59

It seemed like years went by, like a lifetime passed through me . . . and then I woke up. Someone was knocking on the door. I rolled over and bumped into Reese. My head felt like it was full of lead, my arms and legs, too; my whole body ached.

"Hello?" I said to the door, since I was the only one awake.

"It's the manager; open up," said the voice.

I struggled to my feet. I was still dressed. We all were. Harold and Carl weren't even under the covers.

I went to the door. I wasn't sure what to do. I looked out the peephole. It really was the manager. He was short and balding and he was by himself.

I opened the door.

The manager looked me up and down. I squinted back at him. The skies had cleared. The sunlight was so intense I could barely see.

"My wife, uh . . . ," he said. He looked past me into the room. "You got some kind of party going on here?"

"No," I said. "We're just tired. We've been on a long trip."

"Oh," said the manager. "Well, anyways, my wife said she saw some people heading down to the beach this morning. They looked like they were going swimming maybe, but she says they never came back."

"Yeah?" I said. The storm had blown through. The sky was crystal blue. A light breeze moved the few remaining wisps of hair on the manager's head.

"Did any of your group go to the beach?" he asked.

"I'm not sure," I said. "I don't think so."

"Because there's only one way down to the beach and one way up. So if my wife sees someone goin' down there, and they don't come back, you know, not that it's any of our business . . . ," he said, looking into the room again.

I scratched my head. I couldn't think of what to say.

"So none of you went swimming?" he asked.

"No," I said. "I think everyone's still here."

"All right, if you say so. Gotta be out by eleven, though. Unless you want to pay an extra day."

I nodded and shut the door. I turned to Nick and Sheila, sleeping on the bed. They looked like angels. Nick's face was peaceful and the color was back in his cheeks.

I looked at Harold and Carl, fast asleep in their T-shirts and old jeans.

I looked at Reese on the floor. The minute I saw her sleeping face a sob broke out of my chest. I knew who the manager's wife had seen. Steve, Dave, and Mike. They were gone. They'd returned to the ocean.

I wanted to be sure. I walked around the beds and through the connecting doorway. There was only one person left in the other room. My father was asleep in a chair, his head down on his chest. He was breathing evenly, his pipe in his lap. He was probably asking them questions to the last possible moment.

I started to cry. At the same time I desperately searched the room for any last trace of them, any memento, something they had touched or that would prove they'd been there, so I wouldn't forgot them, so all of this wouldn't dissolve into some weird blur in my memory.

There was nothing. The beds hadn't been touched. Everything was exactly as it had been when we checked in.

I went back to the first room and slipped on my Nikes. I pulled on my sweatshirt and stepped over Reese. I let myself out, wiping the tears from my face as I shut the door. The manager was in his little office. I snuck past and ran down the wooden stairs to the beach.

It was a long stairway. Below me, to the right, was about a half mile of smooth beach, to the left a bluff stuck out almost to the water's edge. No one was visible on the beach, but I hurried down anyway.

At the bottom, I ran across the hard sand toward the water. There was no sign of Steve, Dave, or Mike. To my left was the bluff. At the base of it waves were crashing on rocks. There was probably a cove behind it. I ran in that direction and began crawling over the rocks. It was hard climbing and I got splashed by the waves. At one point I fell and skinned my leg.

But I was right; there was a cove. It was small and hidden from the other sections of the beach. And then I saw a person, a man, sitting in the soft sand, by himself, his forearms resting on his knees as he stared at the ocean. I walked casually in that direction. As I got closer, I saw it was Steve.

60

At first I was scared that maybe he wouldn't want me there, but as I got close I felt a calmness come over me. It was Steve, after all; he was my friend; we had been through a lot; we had helped each other.

But he was also like a God. He was like something you couldn't quite believe even existed.

I trudged across the sand. He did not look up. He stared forward.

"Hey, Steve," I said when I reached him. I pulled my hair around one ear.

"Hello, Emily."

"Where are Dave and Mike?"

"They've gone back."

I nodded. I squinted and looked into the surf. There was no sign of anyone.

"Are you going, too?"

"Yes."

I nodded more. "Weren't you even going to say good-bye?" I asked.

"I wanted to. We all did. It's better sometimes to do things quickly and without communication. I've learned that here."

I didn't say anything. I stood there. Neither of us spoke. He saw the cut on my leg. "You hurt yourself," he said.

"I slipped on the rocks."

He put his hand near the wound.

"Can you heal it?" I asked.

"No," he said, taking his hand away. "I have no powers left."

"Will you be able to change back? When you get in the ocean?"

"Yes, because the others are there and they will help me. But right now I am very human. That's why I hesitate. That's why it hurts to go. Now I know why people don't want to die. It's hard to leave this place."

"I know," I said.

He sat staring into the surf. He looked so handsome, like a hero from an ancient time.

I tried to think of something to say. "Sorry about the ocean," I said.

He looked up at me.

"For polluting it and all that," I said. "You know, since you live there and everything."

He smiled. "It's not your fault."

"But it's all our faults, isn't it? Humans, I mean?"

"It's no one's fault. You are a restless species on a planet in constant change. This is your fate. This is your destiny."

I wanted to sit with him. I started to, but then he rocked forward and got to his feet.

My heart collapsed in my chest. "Oh god," I said. Tears again filled my eyes. "I know you have to go. But I don't want you to."

"I feel the same," he said, brushing the sand off his hands. "I feel connected to you, to everyone I have encountered."

"Oh my god!" I gasped, afraid to look at him. "You can't—"

"I have to," he said. He touched my shoulder, leaned forward, and kissed my forehead. I glanced up at him. For the first time I saw how old he was. I saw it in his face. I mean, he still looked like he always did. But suddenly I could see the ages in him, the thousands of years, the millions of years; it was all there, in his eyes, in his face. He was as old as time itself.

He turned and walked toward the surf. I watched him go. He walked across the sand and into the shallow water. I wiped my tears with the sleeves of my sweatshirt. He turned at the waterline and looked at me without expression. Then he stepped deeper into the surf.

I watched him. The breeze blew my hair into my eyes. I had to squint to see, the sun was so bright on the water.

He waded until he was up to his waist. Then he dove

forward and began to swim. I stepped closer to the shore-line, pulling my hair back.

He swam. I watched him. He swam until I could only see his head and shoulders in the surf, then I could only see his head, and then I could only see a small dark spot that was still him. I thought it was; I hoped it was. But eventually there were many black spots and none were him and there was nothing to see anymore, nothing but the beautiful green ocean, the white foam of the surf, the perfect smoothness of the sand at my feet.

He was gone. It was over.

61

I wish I could say that there was some clear warning the aliens transmitted through us, something so profound and urgent it spread across the whole planet and made people stop polluting the oceans or destroying the ozone or whatever. But that's not what happened. Those of us who knew Steve and Dave were so stunned, so completely overwhelmed by what happened, we were like zombies for weeks afterward. Our brains just couldn't process the things we had seen. Sheila, I remember, blocked the whole thing out. She was like *don't talk to me; I just want to go home*. Reese was the same, not denying that it happened but saying it was too much, leave her alone, she just wanted to get back to her normal life. I never even saw Nick again. He was bedridden for a couple of days and his parents got so freaked out they took him to the hospital. When the doctors couldn't find anything wrong with him, Nick and his family all flew back to Australia.

My dad seemed energized at first, he spent a couple days on his computer, but even he gave up eventually. It was just too much. It was too much to know. It was too much to think about. And it wasn't something you could share with anyone. Ironically, the great communicating aliens were not something you could tell your friends about.

The summer people went home. Harold and Carl made themselves scarce. Reese left a week earlier than she had planned to, making up an excuse about getting her college stuff ready for senior year. I seemed to be the only one who wanted to think about Steve and Dave. I was the one who was still hoping something good could come of all this. Surely they had left us something to work with, some clue of what direction we should go in. But they had left nothing. Everything was gone. My dad even threw away his own notes. I couldn't tell if he was doing it to protect me and his career or if he was doing it to preserve his own sanity. It was the same problem we all had. It was too big of a burden. It was better to let it go.

Finally, it was time for me to go back. The morning of my flight I went for a long walk on the beach. It was the end of summer and cloudy and nobody was on the beach. I saw a seagull standing at the shoreline. I approached him hoping to "hear" something, to get some sort of contact, to remember one last time what it was like to know all the life around me.

But there was nothing. He was as mute to me as a rock. The world was a divided place again, where everyone existed separate and alone.

62

I went back to Indianapolis, back to school, back to worrying about tests and boys and what kind of cell phones were cool this year. I slipped back into things easily enough. One thing I did though, I changed several of my electives to science. I just suddenly wanted to know stuff. Like the weather. Or the oceans. Or how currents worked. Or how fish breathed. People were pretty surprised by that, my teachers and my mom especially. They were even more surprised when I aced every test and was soon at the top of the class. I don't know why. I've always been smart. And the science part, I definitely had the genes for that.

Months went by and I lost contact with everyone, even Reese, who I would normally get a couple e-mails from over the course of the school year. Christmas came, and then New Year's, and then in January I got a letter. Not an e-mail, an actual letter, in an envelope. It was from Cape Cod. But it wasn't from my dad. It was from Harold, of all people. I tore it open.

Hi Emily,

I got your address from your dad. I hope you don't mind. I feel a little weird writing to you. But after last summer I figured it would be okay. Not that we're friends exactly. But you know.

Well, the main thing I want to tell you is: Reese is here. She moved back here. She's living in that old house at the end of hotel row. I figured you would know that since you guys are such good friends and stuff. But then I saw her in Antonio's about two weeks ago and she was talking on her cell phone and telling someone that no one knew where she was and she wanted to keep it that way.

Then I saw your dad a couple days after that and I said something about her to him, but he didn't know she was here, either.

So I thought that was a little weird.

Also, she just walks up and down the beach all day. Like she's maybe looking for someone? Like those guys maybe? I mean, nobody around here ever talks about that anymore. Nobody. So nobody will say anything. They just say she's some crazy girl from Boston. Like she's not playing with a full deck or whatever.

So anyway. The only other thing is, well, I feel funny saying this because I'm no expert, but I think she might be pregnant. And my mom saw her walking around and she said that, too. I mean, I don't know much about that sort of thing. But it sorta looks like it.

Just thought you would want to know.

Harold

I read this letter sitting on my bed. I lowered it into my lap when I finished it. My whole body sort of melted in a way. Then I read it again. I read it a third time.

Then I folded it up, hid it under my pillow, and went online to look up plane tickets. . . .

Acknowledgments

Big thanks to my friend, colleague, and fellow amateur philosopher Jonathan Schmidt for first bringing this book to the light of day. Also, big thanks to Susan Chang, Kathleen Doherty, and Jodi Reamer. Special thanks to Beth Rosenberg for readings and support.

About the Author

Blake Nelson lives in Brooklyn, New York. He is the author of many books for children and adults, including *Girl* and *Paranold Park,* soon to be a feature film directed by Gus Van Sant. *They Came from Below* is his first book of science fiction and fantasy.